ALL BY Myself

KEN BACHTOLD

Dreamspinner Press

Published by
DREAMSPINNER PRESS

5032 Capital Circle SW, Suite 2, PMB# 279, Tallahassee, FL 32305-7886 USA
http://www.dreamspinnerpress.com/

All By Myself
© 2015 Ken Bachtold.

Cover Art
© 2015 Reese Dante.
www.reesedante.com
Cover content is for illustrative purposes only and any person depicted on the cover is a model.

ISBN: 978-1-63216-532-9
Digital ISBN: 978-1-63216-533-6
Library of Congress Control Number: 2014953475
First Edition February 2015

Printed in the United States of America
∞
This paper meets the requirements of
ANSI/NISO Z39.48-1992 (Permanence of Paper).

For my dear friend, Vera E. Chazen.

Prologue

MITCH DONNELLY couldn't get that persistent song out of his head. Just when he thought he'd conquered it, he found himself humming the melody again. It wasn't that he didn't like the song, it was just that the lyrics hit too close to home. He'd heard it the day before on his favorite jazz station, and since then it had run repeatedly through his mind, to his continuing distress. Of course, he already knew the song by heart because he and his aunt used to play it—along with "My Merry Oldsmobile" and many others—on thick old disks on a really, really old Victrola, one you actually had to wind up. He remembered the announcer saying, "This is an old song, 'All By Myself,' by Irving Berlin, introduced in 1921." The recording Mitch heard was by Ella Fitzgerald. But Mitch much preferred the original lyrics, just as he and his aunt had sung them repeatedly. The theme, of course, was about being alone. Loneliness was sad, but it was also safe. The trade-off seemed worth it to him. But that old song was probably chuckling at his ire, as it relentlessly kept playing itself in his head. He found himself half humming and half muttering the lyrics.

Yeah, he was all by himself, all right—but it was by choice. He would never, but *never*, let himself get hurt like that again.

...Solitaire... Morris chair...

Of course, he didn't play solitaire, and he didn't have a Morris chair—in fact, he'd never been sure what a Morris chair was, until one day, intrigued, he'd looked it up and found it to be an early version of a reclining chair. An early La-Z-Boy, as it were. Naturally "Morris chair" had been changed, probably because no one now would know what it

1

was. Mitch figured Irving Berlin would agree with him that, just as he had done, they should look it up.

...ticktock...

Mitch thought "ticktock" was a nice touch to describe a clock—clever and a bit of fun. That word altered from the original was what bothered him the most in the version he'd heard on the radio. It was almost like an insult to his memory of his aunt and their many songfests. He'd watched his own "ticktock" for endless hours once upon a time. But he didn't want his thoughts to go there. It had been years since he'd successfully locked that horrible time in his life inside an impenetrable mental box.

...weary head... shoulder...

He really didn't want to finish the song, but it wouldn't let him quit.

...grow older...

"All by myself," he said.

Well, that was the crux of it. Naturally, he'd love to rest his head, weary or not, on somebody's shoulder. And it was hell growing older all alone. If only Jared hadn't—but, no, he was not going to let himself go there. No way. Too much pain.

"It's a beautiful June day," Mitch said firmly and out loud. He didn't care if other strollers thought he was crazy, talking to himself. "I'm here in Central Park, and it's 2010. It's been so many years since I lost Jared. Will I never get over it?" The question hung in the air as if it had substance and weight of its own. He walked on.

Chapter One

MITCH WAS startled out of his reverie when he heard a strange sound. It wasn't a moan, and it wasn't crying, but whatever it was it sounded heartrending. It caused him to shudder, the wild sadness of it. Keening, he decided. That was what it was—keening, like at a traditional wake so often encountered in Irish literature. Such a sad, sad, mournful sound.

He'd been meandering through scattered trees on a grassy hillock in New York's Central Park as he fought his troubled thoughts.... Now he raised his face to the warm touch of the sun. It was a "nice" face, he'd always thought. Dark hair falling over a wide forehead, startling green eyes ("They're really green, aren't they?" driver's license personnel had often remarked), straight nose over full, rather sensuous lips, and a firm chin. More than one person had called him Clark Kent.

"And right this minute, moaning like a big crybaby... better stop," he muttered.

He'd finished his workout at the gym that morning in the usual forty-five minutes. He marveled that more guys didn't know that working out more than that had diminishing returns. When he'd stepped out onto the sidewalk, he'd started walking aimlessly and ended up here in the park. It wasn't gloomy days that got him down, no; it was beautiful, perfect days like this one that seemed the grimmest. That was when sometimes a sudden stab of loneliness shot through him, a feeling, he'd surmised, much like a phantom stiletto. Often it felt like it just might cause him to black out it was so sudden and potent—probably mentally more than physically. But he reminded himself that he couldn't go through that immobilizing loss again. The walls he'd metaphorically built around his heart would have to stay where they were. And he couldn't have it both ways; that was for sure.

By nature, Mitch had always been a very affectionate fellow, but had always been afraid he might give too much of himself away to other men if he didn't curb himself. So throughout much of his early life, Mitch had strangled any attraction to another man. Oh, he'd had what he thought of as furtive, secret liaisons early on, but he'd always come away feeling more isolated than before—and dissatisfied. Mitch never went searching without secretly hoping he might meet the proverbial "Mr. Right." Then he'd have a perfectly valid reason to come out, and he'd be able to take whatever fallout followed. However, that gentleman had proved very elusive. He wanted to feel he couldn't exist without that magical person, and that same person couldn't exist without him. Mitch wanted—he probably wanted too much. But then he'd met Jared.

He'd loved Jared. Oh, how he had loved Jared! Maybe a guy only gets one "Mr. Right" in a lifetime. At twenty-four, flinging caution to the wind, he'd plunged into love like a cliff diver into the ocean. Holding nothing back, he'd given himself wholly to a sweetheart of a guy. Denying it now wouldn't help, wouldn't keep the thoughts of what happened from escaping a little from that barred cell in his mind.

After losing Jared, he'd felt nothing for many years. Then, tentatively, he'd begun going out once again. But always with a certain caution, always holding back a bit of himself. That it was self-defense made no difference. He couldn't seem to stop feeling that he'd only suffer great loss once again. This probably conveyed itself to the guys he met, because, invariably, they seemed to drift away and disappear. And to be truthful, he'd really not cared that much. No one ever caused him to feel remotely like he'd felt about Jared.

And he'd told himself again, as he often did, that loneliness was better than loss. And, of course, that always made him think of Jared. After all this time, it was still too painful to go there very often, so he tried to think of other things. He tried to think of current events, or about trying, perhaps, to be more aggressive about finding a second "Mr. Right."

In fact, lately he'd become something of a recluse, not wanting to be disappointed again. He'd spent most of his time writing his fairly successful novels. But sometimes his nice little apartment on Perry Street in the West Village got rather claustrophobic, and he had to get out. Like today.

He'd been walking slowly, hearing the crunch of the dry grass under his feet and feeling the slight breeze on his skin. The lovely earthy smell of the trees and shrubs permeated the air. It really was a beautiful day, complete with a couple of lazy clouds, one in the shape of an elephant, meandering across the almost unreal blue sky. He just had to get hold of himself and go on. What else could he do? So, in better spirits, he'd trudged on.

Now, he shuddered again as he heard that strange primal wail cutting through the myriad sounds of the day. Though not loud in sound, it was fearful in emotion.

He started to walk on, figuring it was none of his business, and he shouldn't intrude, whatever it was. But after a few steps, he couldn't seem to move. Something or somebody was in deep trouble. He finally stepped off into the cluster of bushes, parting branches here and there, and soon looked down the hill and saw a man's form clutching the earth like he wanted to dig right into it. Then came that awful sound, softer now, almost beyond hearing, but just as forlorn. The guy seemed to be trembling mightily. Was he sick? What could be so horrible as to provoke that sound?

Mitch stepped slowly forward and crossed over to the man. At first he didn't know quite what to do. This was a stranger, after all, and maybe he wanted to be alone in his grief. But then some strange force caused him to sit down and reach out to touch the broad shoulders that somehow seemed so fragile. He pulled his hand back, but then forced himself to lay it on the tense muscles in cautious little pats. He heard himself saying softly, "It's okay. It's okay. I'm here." Why this should be soothing, he didn't know, but somehow it seemed to work, and he felt the man relax a bit.

He moved his hand in ever-widening circles until he was patting and soothing from shoulder to waist. In an abstract way he felt the strength of the muscles beneath his hand, but he was so concerned with offering comfort that the sensation didn't register. He massaged the poor guy's neck and ran his hand through the tangled, dark brown curls. He remembered the time when, as a child, he'd had the measles and was in a darkened room, and his older brother had threaded his fingers through his hair, and how soothing it had been.

He suddenly became aware of the entire form beneath him: long Levi's-clad legs, an incredibly small waist, and broad shoulders. Beautiful hair. But, he mused, probably the face of a bulldog. As if it mattered, anyway.

The man, quiet now, turned on his side and looked up at Mitch. Not a bulldog at all. In fact, what ran through his mind as he looked down at the face before him was, "Hollywood Material." Huge blue eyes, though red-rimmed, and even, perfectly symmetrical features. The guy was handsome personified. That startled Mitch more than anything else. It was so unexpected. He felt a strange stirring in his chest, much like the feeling when the roller coaster tops the first hill and starts down. It caught him unprepared and caused him to wonder what was happening to him.

"S-sorry," the guy said. "I—I'm so sorry to be such a mess. I'm so—so embarrassed to fall apart like this. I'm usually the strong, stoic type."

"We can't be strong and stoic all the time," Mitch told him. "In my own way, I've been in the same sort of place you seem to be in now, so I do understand."

"Oh," he replied, trying to raise himself and failing; he grimaced and closed his eyes tightly. Mitch drew him up against his chest, resumed the soothing backrub, and said again, "It's okay. I'm here for you. It's okay."

He really didn't know what he meant by those words, but he knew they were true. Stranger or no stranger, this guy seemed important to him. Figure that. In a short time he realized the fellow, worn out, had fallen asleep. Mitch lay back on the ground, hearing the fallen leaves crunch beneath him, still holding on to the limp figure. The crushed leaves gave off an earthy fragrance that filled the air around him. He realized that what he felt in addition to concern was contentment. This felt so good, just holding someone, nothing further expected nor wanted, just the delight of the strong body pressing against his own. He smiled. It wasn't long before he fell asleep too.

He woke when he felt the other man stirring. As they sat up, they looked at each other almost in surprise, like, "Where am I?" And, "Who is this?" It all seemed to come back to them at the same time, and they gave each other rather lopsided grins—or were they grimaces?

"Ye gods," said Mitch, trying to lighten the moment. "Here we've slept together, and we don't even know each other's name." This remark resulted in a wan smile, but a smile nevertheless.

"My name is Grady. Grady Gilmore," the stranger said. "My mother was into alliteration when I was born." He drew away, just a bit reluctantly, Mitch realized.

"Hi, Grady. I'm Mitch Donnelly."

"Hi, Mitch," he said.

"Do you want to talk about it? I'm a good listener. And I think it's always a good idea to vent."

"Could we just talk platitudes for a bit? Then, if you still want me to, I'll tell you all about it."

"Sure," Mitch replied. "Ah—where are you from? How's that for a platitude?"

"Perfect. I'm originally from Berkeley—well, actually, Oakland, in the hills, but we always said Berkeley. My family thought it sounded more high-class, more intellectual. And then I lived in San Francisco for a while."

"Such a beautiful city. I lived there for a time when I was in college. What brought you to New York?"

"My...." He stumbled and then said hoarsely, "My partner—my partner got a job offer, and I, of course, came too. Where are you from originally, Mitch?" he added quickly.

"I'm not a native New Yorker either. I come from the wine country in California, the Sonoma Valley. I also met someone very important to me in San Francisco during college. And yet," Mitch added, "here we are crossing paths all the way across the country, far from the West Coast, in Central Park, on the side of a hill in New York. What are the chances? Sorry about the circumstances, though."

"I have to confess, since, as you say, we've slept together, that it was an easy decision for me to come to New York because of the lure of the big time. I was a theater major at San Francisco State, and when Hank—that's his name—got this promotion and relocation, I thought I'd come to New York and dazzle Broadway."

"And—"

"Broadway dazzled me, instead."

"How so?"

"Well, I thought I was kind of unique." Grady seemed to relax somewhat when talking about theater. "But when I walked into my first audition, there were literally hundreds of people and, seemingly, at least a hundred looked just like me—or at least my type. My third audition got me a callback, though. I figured, well, maybe this is going to work out after all. But I was highly nervous. It was a singing audition for a big musical."

Mitch watched Grady pick up a leaf and slowly trace the veining with a forefinger. "So you sing too?"

"Well, that's debatable. I took six years of singing lessons, but I was never secure. You see, when I was twelve, I was in a church choir—oh, I'm hardly the religious type—but all my friends were in the choir, so I joined too. One day the choir director, a rather insensitive old bat, said, 'Grady, I think you'd better go home, and come back when your voice finishes changing.'"

"Oh, that was cruel."

"Devastating at twelve, and in front of all my friends. So I went home, and I never set foot in the church again. Or any other, actually."

"Don't blame you."

"So, anyway, I had this audition—they wanted a ballad, and my singing teacher at the time and I decided I would knock them dead with my version of 'My Funny Valentine.'"

"Great song."

"Yes," Grady answered as a grimace crossed his face. "But I was so nervous that my knees were actually shaking. So I started out okay, but then toward the end, where the notes go up and up, I started to go sharp, and I couldn't stop myself. And I went sharper and sharper.

Painful. I wondered if maybe it wasn't as bad as I thought, but when I left the room, the other actors all looked at the floor. I didn't go to another audition for several weeks. I was afraid I'd run into someone who'd heard me."

"Poor guy," Mitch told him, and without thinking, he patted his shoulder, but then felt a delicious shiver at the contact. This was a no-no, he told himself. This was trouble. This was a guy in some emotional turmoil and definitely not available. Pity, he thought. He seemed so nice, in addition to being so good-looking. Grady's beautiful brown hair now had golden highlights from the slowly setting sun, which Mitch found captivating. He watched his fingers toying with the leaf. Long-fingered, they looked like a musician's hands. Perhaps he played some instrument as well as singing. Ye gods, was he feeling real bona fide attraction? After all this time?

"I do some acting now and then," Grady went on, "mostly showcase stuff, and a couple of fantastic roles out at a couple of community theaters in New Jersey. I got to do Salieri in *Amadeus*, Garry Essendine in *Present Laughter*, and Weller Martin in *The Gin Game*."

"What do you do for—what shall I call it—stay-alive money?"

"I do PowerPoint presentations at a law firm. To impress their clients, and for court displays, et cetera. I had an art minor, so it's not too terrible."

"But not what you love."

"No, but you do what you have to do, right?"

"Right."

"And you, Mitch?"

"I write mildly successful novels. Enough to live on, but I'm still waiting for the big best seller."

"So, are we a couple of thwarted artists?"

"I'd say we have that in common."

Then a lengthy silence followed. Mitch was aware of the twittering of birds and muted conversations from far off. He could barely hear the tiny calliope music of the merry-go-round over by the zoo. The sun sat lower in the sky, shadows elongated, and the air turned a bit cooler. Time seemed to have fled by.

"Do you feel like talking about it now?" Mitch asked gently.

9

"No. But I think you deserve to know, since you probably saved my sanity."

Mitch felt himself blushing. He was not one to blush. What was up with him? What was going on here?

"Aw—" he started.

"You're a good guy, Mitch. You know that?"

Mitch could only smile in return. He didn't quite know what to say.

"All right, here goes," Grady began. "Get ready for cliché time."

"What time?"

"Cliché. What I'm about to tell you is such a cliché."

"Okay."

"Have you ever been in a committed, long-term relationship, Mitch?"

"Certainly not long-term, but committed while it lasted."

"That's sad."

"The best period of my life led to the worst, actually." Here he was admitting highly personal facts to a virtual stranger—and rather comfortably. What was that all about? Perhaps because they'd shared such raw emotions together. It had just slipped out. Usually he was more guarded about his personal life and the huge empty space it contained.

"But," Mitch added, "you were going to tell me whatever happened to cause you such grief. We can discuss my hang-ups some other time."

After a strangely intense stare, Grady simply said, "Yes, we will." He paused, then said, "Imagine this. You've been with one person literally since birth. Your mothers were college roommates. Had a double wedding when they graduated and settled down next to each other. You and he actually shared the same playpen. Started kindergarten together. Inseparable through high school. You've discovered you love each other along the way in your teenage years, to great delight, and have been together ever since."

"I envy you." Just what he'd always dreamed about—finding, once again, one guy to bond with completely. A true reason for living. Something he'd vaguely hoped for beginning a couple of years or so after the accident, albeit timidly, but had never found. Had never even come close. But that was another story.

"You might not envy me when you hear the whole story," Grady said, his voice almost a whisper.

"You don't need to go on if you'd rather not."

"No, I think it'll help me to get it all out. Maybe some of the angst will lessen." This time his smile was almost genuine. Small, but there.

"Okay."

"To go on, then, picture coming home to the condo you've shared here in New York for over five years."

"All right, I think I've got the picture." Mitch adjusted his position, so they were now facing each other squarely. The sun was much lower in the sky, and the slanting rays seemed to put a glow around the hollow in which they were talking. Due to this new angle, Mitch was able to see through the foliage to where a young couple was walking along the path he'd been taking when he'd first heard Grady's sorrowful sounds. They made a pretty picture, she in a yellow summer dress and he in a dark green polo shirt. The only reason Mitch was able to see their little dog was because it was being held up in the air by the young man and was wiggling and barking happily. They all seemed so carefree. What a contrast to the atmosphere down here with Grady. Close proximity, but worlds apart. He became aware that Grady was continuing, after a lengthy pause, with his sad tale.

"I'd gotten off work early, and I stopped for some wine and flowers for him. Tulips. Red tulips. I did things like that. It never ceased to be fun to imagine the look on his face when I brought presents home. I think I got more pleasure out of giving him things than he did in receiving them. Every so often he brought me the same sort of things. In many ways we're much alike." A pause. "Some things—not so much."

"That's sounds so nice. I've never had anyone bring me wine—or flowers," Mitch replied.

"Anyway, I snuck up to our door, took out my key, and quietly turned the lock. I didn't want him to hear me. When I got inside, I closed the door slowly and crept forward. There was no one in the living room, but I heard Hank chuckling over something in our bedroom. I figured he must be on the phone, so I snuck to the door and pushed it open." He stopped suddenly and his eyes filled with tears.

"You don't need to go on. I think I get the picture."

"No," Grady managed hoarsely, "let me go on. There he was—there he was, naked, lying on top of some... some guy and kissing him—passionately. I think it was the kissing that got me most. It's the most intimate, the most personal thing. It looked like afterglow time, the deed, as it were, having been done."

"Oh, God," Mitch said, "how devastating."

"That—that's the perfect word. I saw black swirls, like clouds, just like you read about, and thought I was going to pass out. I dropped the flowers and the wine, which promptly burst open on the floor in a giant spray of red. It sounded like an explosion. I probably said something, but I don't know what it was. The other guy grabbed his clothes, pushed me aside, and ran out the front door, still naked! Probably startled any neighbors, if they were in the hall."

"Undoubtedly."

"Hank started some kind of explanation, but it was just garbled noise to me. I don't think I could have been more surprised if he'd come at me with a knife. This sure wasn't the Hank I knew, or thought I knew."

"After all that time?"

"Yeah, how about that. When he got up and came toward me, I shoved him as hard as I could, and he fell back on the bed. I slammed out of the condo and started running. First down the stairs—couldn't wait for the elevator—then down the street. I just kept running until I couldn't anymore, and then I just stumbled along. I really don't remember much else until I looked up later to see you trying to comfort me."

They stared at each other for a long time.

"And here we are," Grady said.

"And here we are," Mitch replied. He stood up and raised Grady to his feet as well. "What are you going to do now?"

The sky had darkened; it was the time of day that Jared had always called *L'heure bleu*—the Blue Hour. *Entre chien et loup* was, perhaps, more accurate. Dusk, as it were. There was, indeed, a blue cast to Grady's face, outlining his strong cheekbones and a slight cleft in his chin. Crickets had decided to start an impromptu concert, taking over from the many birds that had been singing throughout the day. Mitch shivered. It was suddenly chilly.

"I'm certainly not going back to the condo—at least, not for a while. I suppose I'll go to some hotel. Or maybe to our national shrine."

"National shrine?"

"You know, the YMCA."

"I don't think so."

"What do you mean?" Grady asked, puzzled.

"Look, Grady, we really don't know each other well, but an experience like we've just been through together is like knowing each other for years. I have a spare room at my place, and I think you should come home with me and stay for a while."

"No. I've already leaned on you far too much. That would be imposing."

"Not at all. I don't want you to be alone and start getting upset again." When Grady started to protest, Mitch went on. "Besides, I think you owe it to me to hear my life story."

Grady just shook his head. But then he looked up and nodded.

To his surprise Mitch felt great relief. He realized he would have been very disappointed to have this encounter end here. There wasn't time to analyze his feelings, as Grady started walking down the hill; his shoes made squeaking noises in the grass. Mitch followed, feeling a strange mix of emotions.

Chapter Two

THE CAB ride down Seventh Avenue to the West Village was a very colorful one as they shot through the Forty-Second Street area, with its constantly moving and changing lights, almost psychedelic in its intensity. The huge screens and moving lights were dizzying if you looked too long. Past Madison Square Garden, and the Pennsylvania Hotel. Past the seemingly endless string of banks, the countless Starbucks, the Gap stores, which seemed to spring up like mushrooms. As they zoomed by FIT (the Fashion Institute of Technology) at the corner of Twenty-Seventh Street, Mitch couldn't help looking at the odd sculpture there, which always reminded him of a strange sort of basketball about to be thrown through a misshapen hoop. However, in his opinion, it was far from the worst outdoor sculpture in New York. Take, for instance, the squat lump at the front of the Drama Library at Lincoln Center that was supposed to be a bear, or one of the monstrosities on Park Avenue or that thing that looked like tinfoil at Forth-Second and Third Avenue next to the Gap store. There was only one outdoor sculpture that Mitch thought was worthy of the name and that was the one at Twenty-Ninth and Park Avenue—*The Graceful Ovals*, he'd always called them.

They went past Twenty-Third, a main artery, home of both Home Depot and P.C. Richards, playgrounds of home improvement and electronic devices, respectively. Mitch could spend hours in either of them, like most people would in a museum.

Past Fourteenth Street, with Papaya King on one corner, and the Vitamin Shoppe on the other. Mitch was a favorite customer at the Vitamin Shoppe, where he bought a great deal of his supplements and his protein powder.

After they finally swung to the curb at Perry Street, Mitch paid the driver. As the cab roared away down Seventh Avenue, Mitch guided Grady down the street, wondering if Grady was in any shape to wonder at the long-closed doors of the Perry Street Theatre, home of the first production of David Drake's *The Night Larry Kramer Kissed Me*. Past the silent trees at curbside, looking like late-night sentinels, and the brownstones on the other side, especially the one with the two stone squirrels standing guard on the pedestals at the foot of the banister and, eventually, into his building and up to his second-floor apartment. Once inside he heaved a sigh of relief. The main room had twelve-foot ceilings, with an elaborate curve from the ceiling above down to the top of the walls. It was painted a warm beige, with dark brown trim, the furniture an odd mix that somehow came together to form a den-like feeling. A sofa in off-white canvas, two side chairs to match, a working fireplace with a carved mantel above. Centered there between two Christofle candlesticks was a beautiful dark red Murano glass bowl he'd ordered from the Smithsonian catalog. Large windows extended on either side with heavy velvet dark brown drapes framing them, and a Tiffany-style floor lamp stood beside one of the chairs near a side table, which was loaded with books, both on top, and on a shelf below. A small, slightly worn but intricately patterned Oriental rug partially covered the gleaming parquet floor. A long narrow bench of Asian origin served as the coffee table.

Mitch watched Grady take in his surroundings. For some reason it was important to him that Grady approve of his choices, for he knew his tastes were rather unorthodox.

"Wow. Unique. I'm impressed."

Somehow Mitch had guessed he would approve. He nodded with satisfaction. That reaction told him they most likely had similar tastes.

When Mitch had gotten Grady settled in his spare room, dominated by a king-size sleigh bed and a wall-to-wall beige sculpted carpet, he found a huge towel for Grady and insisted he take a long shower. He was glad he'd set out lavender-scented diffuser sticks, so the guest room, which also housed his Vectra all-purpose gym, wasn't replete with *odor de gym*.

"Wow, what a great setup you have here," Grady said.

"I use it when I'm too busy to get to the gym." Digging in one of the drawers where he kept his many sets of extra gym clothes—he was almost embarrassed about how much he liked different colors on different days—Mitch pulled out a set of sweats and handed them to Grady.

"I still feel like I'm imposing on you. Now you're even giving me your clothes."

"I have enough workout clothes that I'll hardly miss a set. And yours are covered in grass stains," Mitch told him. "Now go and stand under a hot shower for a nice long time. It'll help a lot, I think, and I'll have some dinner for us when you're through." Grady nodded, accepted the clothes and towel, and disappeared into the bathroom.

Mitch moved on to the kitchen, which he'd painted a soft yellow—kitchens should always be yellow, in his opinion—with a Jackson Pollock type linoleum on the floor, heavily spattered with multiple colors, predominantly gold. The appliances were all white and included his most valued pieces—a microwave, and a blender. The microwave was important because Mitch had decided long ago that a person spent a lot of time creating food, a very short time eating it, and a long time cleaning it up. It just wasn't worth it. The blender he needed for his daily protein mixes. The refrigerator was stocked with organic items, and his shelves held whole-grain cereals—anything by Kashi was great with him, particularly the Crunch line. He'd always remarked that if he couldn't peel it or open it, he didn't eat it.

Mitch called for a pizza to be delivered—he wasn't always fanatical in his eating habits, and this was quick, and also the best comfort food he could think of. After the pizza came, he mixed up a couple of protein drinks—good for energy.

When Grady finally emerged from the shower, Mitch couldn't help but notice how well he filled out Mitch's clothes. While he was not as built up as Mitch, he filled the T-shirt very nicely, very cut and muscular. And the sweatpants hung on a very narrow waist.

"Better?" Mitch managed over a catch in his throat.

"Much, but I feel even more embarrassed about breaking down in front of you. What a weakling you must think I am."

ALL BY MYSELF

"Not a bit," Mitch assured him. "As I mentioned, I've been where you are. I know how it feels."

"And...."

"Maybe some other time. Now, come along, I have some—sustenance—for us," he announced grandly.

"Hey, what's with the grandiloquence? I'm supposed to be the actor."

Mitch chuckled as they sat at his built-in breakfast nook and shared the savory-smelling pizza—lots of tomatoes and broccoli, Mitch's favorite. More accurately, Mitch ate pizza while Grady took a few bites and then pushed the rest around his plate. He did, however, drink the protein mix Mitch insisted he swallow. That, at least, would keep him fueled. Mitch had such a drink morning and night—"feeding his muscles," he called it.

"Thank heavens it's Friday," Grady said. "I'll have two whole days to get myself together for work. If I had to go in tomorrow, it would be hard."

"Maybe you ought to call in sick for a day or two. I imagine Hank will try to reach you to explain and smooth things over—unless, that is, at some level you might like him to."

"No way," Grady said. "I'll just have to get over him, even if it kills me. How could I ever trust him again? And he's made me feel like such a fool, such a loser, for being so stupid."

"It's not stupid to trust someone. How could you possibly know it was misplaced, when you'd known each other since childhood? I think everyone needs to have at least one person they can feel confident in trusting totally—if that's possible."

"Do you have someone like that, Mitch?" he asked.

"Umm, not really. I used to, years ago. But not anymore."

"What—"

"Some other time, remember?"

"Sorry, I won't press. I just feel so selfish, only talking about myself and my problems."

"At the moment, Grady, I think that's the most important thing. My stuff can wait until a better time."

"Okay, but promise. I really need to return the favor. You've been so kind to me."

It had been so easy! Mitch was startled by how quickly this thought ran skittering across his mind, but he kept it from showing on his face. To Grady he said, "Later, I promise."

Grady yawned mightily, putting his hand over his mouth. As yawns would, this caused Mitch to yawn also.

"I think it's bedtime. Isn't there some famous line by Shakespeare about sleep knitting up the raveled sleeve of care, or something like that?"

"Yes. But Shakespeare also wrote, 'To sleep, perchance to dream, aye, there's the rub.' *Hamlet*."

"Didn't I tell you?" Mitch said, drawing Grady to his feet and guiding him to the spare room. "This is a dream-free bedroom. Specially built."

Grady stopped suddenly and turned to face Mitch. "I'll have to go back and get my clothes and things." The look on his face would be exactly the same, Mitch decided, if a complicated root canal were in order. "I'll have to be sure he isn't there. I really don't want to run into him now."

"Is there ever a time when you know he won't be there? Some kind of routine he has?"

"He's usually out playing volleyball on the weekends. He's devoted to that game and to his team."

"Do you know where he plays?"

"Yeah, usually in Central Park. I joined in a couple of times, but I just wanted to have fun, and these guys play for blood. So I stopped going."

Mitch was leaning against the doorjamb. "We could swing by and see if he's there—from a distance, of course—and if he is, then we go for it."

Grady looked up with surprise. "You'd go with me?"

"Of course. I'm not about to let you go back there without backup. Not because of him, but because I don't want you to face being there alone."

"Thanks, Mitch—so much." His tone said more than his words.

Mitch felt that tug in his throat once again as he nodded and turned away, then went to his room.

Mitch had trouble going to sleep for some reason. Somehow Grady had provoked a sense of connection, but also a great sense of fear. Fear of loss. He was in a kind of stuporous half sleep when he heard his name whispered softly. He raised his head from his pillow to see Grady standing, forlorn, in his doorway. Without thinking, he lifted the edge of his covers, and Grady covered the space between them like a comet and slid in next to him.

"I don't want to be alone," Grady said softly. "I'm sorry."

"Don't be. I understand."

As they settled down, Grady seemed to nearly pass out. Uh-oh. This could be a very dangerous situation.

He was definitely not into rebound romance—if that was where this could be leading. In fact, he was leery of romance at all; it raised his fears to greater heights. Not that he thought Grady had such a thing in mind, but Mitch could feel himself wanting to get closer, to touch. This was not good. He'd have to be very careful not to let his emotions get out of hand. That he was a lonesome guy, he knew. That Grady was a very handsome guy, a very nice guy, he knew. This was not a good combination. But he couldn't renege on his offer of the spare room. Of course, Grady needing the comfort of a warm body beside him was undoubtedly a one-night thing. Grady was still recovering from a severe shock, that was all. And he, himself, was responding to a nice, good-looking man. This was only natural, he told himself. He was not going to worry about it.

MITCH WOKE up the next morning with a strange weight on his right shoulder. He glanced down and saw Grady's head resting there. He looked so carefree in his sleep. Nobody would guess the turmoil he'd been through the day before. A wave of tenderness passed over Mitch, as if he could, by wishing, keep Grady from hurting so badly. And this after knowing the guy for less than a day? He slipped out of bed without waking Grady, who he figured would be better off asleep than awake at this point. In the kitchen, after mixing the chocolate (his favorite) protein powder and the skim milk in the blender, he switched it on the lowest speed. It hummed along, taking a bit longer to mix than when it ran at its usually fastest, but much louder, speed.

As he was pouring the thick mixture into a glass, he heard a shuffling noise behind him and turned to see a tousled Grady standing in the doorway, running his hand through his hair.

"Morning," he said. He leaned back against the counter and took another sip of his drink.

"Hi," Grady said in a low, hoarse voice. Probably all that crying and talking had roughed up his throat. "Do you still think it's a good idea for me to stay here? If you don't, I'll understand. Impulse of the moment, and all that."

Mitch put his glass down on the counter and crossed to the other man. He put his hands on Grady's shoulders and waited until Grady looked up at him.

"Number one, I don't go back on my promises. Number two, I like having you here. Truth be known, I get lonely a lot of the time— the writer's curse. It is, after all, called the 'Lonely Art.' I was just thinking how nice it is to have company. Though I'm sorry about the reason."

Grady continued to look at him. Then he smiled and nodded. "Okay."

Mitch squeezed his shoulders. "Don't make me get tough with you." He crossed back and, after picking up his glass, finished in one gulp.

"You're a toughie, all right."

"Grrrrr."

Grady chuckled. A real chuckle. That was an improvement.

"Before we go out marauding for your stuff, what would you like for breakfast? I have oatmeal, dry cereal, eggs."

"Would eggs be okay? If it's not too much fuss?"

"I'll have some with you. I have eggs at least a couple times a week. After all that talk about cholesterol, new research finds that there's enough good stuff in the white to counteract the bad stuff in the yolk. That's science for you, always changing its mind. Like chocolate. First it was bad for you, and then, if dark, it's good for you. And wine. First it was not so good, then it was terrific. Who can guess what's next?"

"I couldn't give up chocolate," Grady said, "but I always liked dark chocolate best, so I was okay after all."

"Me too. Most people like milk chocolate."

"Yuck."

"Yuck."

Later, as they ate their eggs, which Mitch had scrambled and cooked in the microwave, with some whole wheat pita bread, Mitch asked, "So are you still thinking of going to work on Monday?"

"Yes, I think I've got a handle on things now, thanks in large part to you. I'm still pretty raw, but it was the utter shock that did it. I'd planned on going to a few auditions this week, and I think I'll just go ahead and do it. Try to keep things as normal as possible. It'll take my mind off things."

"Good idea. Do they let you off work to go to auditions?"

"Yes, I'm really lucky. I can go almost whenever I want, as long as I make up the time either at night or over the weekend. For a would-be actor, this is heaven. Rigid working hours are a killer. Auditions are usually in the daytime, and rehearsals are usually at night. So most actors can only have temp jobs. Scratch any waiter or waitress in New York and you'll find an actor, or a dancer, underneath. Same with bartenders."

"Not easy."

"No. It takes real determination. Or stupidity."

"It must be the first in your case, because you're certainly not the second."

They exchanged a look that held a bit longer than the quip warranted.

Mitch finally looked away and gathered the dishes and put them in the sink.

"I'm going to wash these. The dishwasher is being temperamental."

He started to run water into the sink and got a bottle of liquid soap out of the cupboard underneath. He was thinking over his reaction to Grady and wondering what he was going to do about it, and so concentrated on the problem that he poured an exceedingly generous amount of soap into the running water. It promptly foamed up and began to run over the sink onto the floor.

"Dammit," he muttered, hating to look so foolish in front of Grady. He looked up to see his new friend trying desperately to suppress a smile. But when a chuckle escaped, nevertheless, Mitch couldn't help joining in, and soon they were both laughing out loud. Mitch grabbed some paper towels and scooped up the offending suds with a wry look at Grady. The look seemed to go on and on, neither one wanting to look away.

How long it might have lasted, they would never know, because suddenly the little three-note melody of Mitch's doorbell chimed, followed by two sharp knocks.

"Can you get that for me, Grady? That's Em's special ring," Mitch said. "As you will notice, I'm almost up to my neck in soapsuds."

"Sure." Grady left the kitchen, followed after a few moments by Mitch, who was madly brushing soapsuds from his elbows to his wrists with a towel. He watched Grady cross to the door and swing it open to find a diminutive lady standing there. Five feet tall, if that, with a beautifully coifed helmet of blonde hair (too perfect to be real), a red flannel shirt stuffed into worn jeans, and scuffed brown loafers. She was holding a beribboned little package in her hands and looked up at him in great surprise.

"And who are you?" she asked.

"My name's Grady, ma'am. Grady Gilmore. I'm staying with Mitch for a while."

"Well, good," she replied, sliding agilely past him into the room. "I'm Em Latimore, his landlady—and friend. I must say it's good to see him having company at last. It's about time!"

Mitch strode into the room as Grady shut the door.

"Grady's just a friend," Mitch stated quickly, afraid Em would get the wrong idea.

"Well, hello there, handsome," Em said. "You're looking even better than when I left. Probably because of having a guest, is what I'd surmise. And I notice that maroon is today's color scheme."

Though a bit wet, Mitch wore his usual sweatpants, wine-colored today, with a sleeveless T-shirt that matched, his hair a tangle of black curls.

22

Mitch dropped the towel he was carrying onto the nearest table. On the highly polished hardwood floor, he slipped on sock-clad feet around the sofa and over to Em in three giant slides. He picked her right up off the floor and twirled her around several times.

"Welcome home," he sang in an off-key little melody. "Welcome home, home, home at last from the sea."

"Put me down, you great beast," she said indignantly. "You're going to make me dizzy, and you might knock my hair off."

Mitch set her down and then gave her a big hug. "I missed you. I actually missed you scolding me all the time."

"Well," she said pointedly, looking at Grady, "looks like some of my advice finally took."

"Emma," Mitch said hastily, "this is Grady Gilmore. Grady, this is my dear friend and landlady, Emma Latimore."

"Redundant," Emma said.

"What?"

"The introduction is redundant. We've already introduced ourselves. Isn't that right, young man?"

"Sure is, ma'am."

"And please call me Em. Ma'am makes me feel like an old lady."

"If the shoe fits," Mitch mumbled.

"Now don't you start. I'm in much too good a mood to bandy verbal swords with you. Besides, you know I always win."

"True," Mitch admitted. Mitch watched Grady smile at the good-natured banter. He realized Grady must have caught the almost familial feeling between him and Em, and he was pleased at the knowing look he saw in Grady's eyes.

"It looks like you brought Mitch a present," Grady said.

"Yes, though he hardly deserves it. Twirling me around like a top, indeed."

"I was just overcome with delight at having you back," Mitch explained. "Em's been gone on a cruise," he said to Grady. He led them to the sofa and then sat in the chair opposite. As they sat down, Em offered the present to Mitch.

"Two weeks," she told Grady. "Two weeks on a big yacht with about a thousand old ladies. It was like a geriatric Olivia cruise."

"But did you meet anyone?" Mitch asked. "That, as you told me when you booked the cruise, was supposedly your mission."

She turned to Grady. "Unlike someone we know, I don't believe in drying up on the vine of life, if I may wax poetic."

"You should know that Emma taught English literature for many years," Mitch told Grady. "Hence the purple prose you hear from time to time."

"Well, at least I'm not stagnating. You know what my Caroline meant to me. I loved that woman dearly for over thirty years. But she wouldn't want me to go on mourning forever, just like I wouldn't have wanted that for her if the situation were reversed."

"I know, Em, you two were the poster girls for commitment. I know that better than anyone. I'd never belittle the bond you had."

"I know, dear. I just want you to get back into life. The accident must have been a terrible thing for you, but as they say, life goes on. You're too good a soul not to have a partner. Someone deserves you, I think."

Mitch looked anxiously at Grady to see how he was taking these revelations. He hadn't as yet divulged his past, as he'd promised to do. Too painful, even now. This would bring the whole issue up front once again. He met a sharp gaze from Grady's blue eyes. They seemed to say, "You promised, and now you have no excuse to hold back."

The look he shot back implied, "Later, I promise."

"But what's this you brought me?" he said quickly to bridge the awkward moment.

"Well, wouldn't that spoil the surprise, if I told you. Just open the package."

Mitch did as he was told, and after disposing of the shiny gold wrapping paper and brilliant red ribbon, he held up a beautiful box of chocolates.

"Wow. If I didn't have an audience, there would be teeth marks on this box, because I couldn't wait to get at the goodies!"

"Those are Belgian chocolates. Very posh. Dark, of course. The very best for the biggest chocolate lover I know. Not counting me!"

"I truly love it. You know I'm a chocolate fiend or you wouldn't have picked this."

"I can vouch for that," Grady said, obviously remembering their discussion about the virtues of dark chocolate with a lot of cocoa versus milk chocolate.

"But now I'm going to want chocolate every time I look at the box."

"Live with it. It'll strengthen your willpower," Em said as she rose. "I have to go. I'm having lunch with Sarah."

"Sarah who?" Mitch almost shouted. "I thought you didn't meet anyone."

"I didn't say anything about not making a friend."

"I'll be watching you," Mitch called out as she slipped out the door.

"If you're fast enough," she shot back as the door swung shut.

Mitch hurried to the door and pulled it back open, revealing the hall's freshly painted cream-colored walls and the black-and-white octagonal tiled floor. Just as Emma was about to descend the stairway, he called after her, "Are you going to be home this afternoon? And if so, can I borrow the car? We need to get Grady's stuff from… from—from wherever it is."

"Interesting choice of words there, my boy," Em replied, turning back, one hand on the worn but highly waxed wood of the banister. "I sense a story, but I won't push. You'll tell me when you're ready—you always do."

"Unfortunately, you're right. You're a terrific listener. Would it be okay if we stop by a little later for the keys?"

"Sure, as long as you're not going to some remote spot—to commune with nature, that is."

"Emma, this is strictly business," he complained.

"Right," she said and chuckled, her shoes making an accompanying tattoo until she was out of sight.

"Well, she's something else," Grady said as Mitch closed the door.

"It would take the UN to deal with her properly," Mitch said, "but she's been a wonderful friend to me. We've become almost like family."

25

Grady smiled the smile that always seemed to unsettle Mitch, saying, "I saw that right away. She must miss her friend, so it's nice she has you to turn to."

"You should have seen those two women. What a pair. Caroline was quite tall. Probably five foot ten at least and every inch the lady. Gloves, hat, and purse always matching. And you've just witnessed Emma. But, oh, did they care about each other."

"What's with the wig?"

"Emma had beautiful hair as a young woman. Then she almost died of scarlet fever. She recovered, but her hair was never the same. She has a set of beautiful wigs in various styles and colors, but she wears that horrible one, sort of like a dust cap, when she's doing housework and such. It's her one vanity. But as long as I've known her, I've never seen her without one of her wardrobe of wigs."

After a bit of silence, Grady spoke. "I think it's finally time for you to tell me about your past. You know, I showed you mine, you show me yours? You did promise, and you've been dodging the issue."

Mitch smiled, though with much trepidation.

Grady curled up on one end of the sofa, and Mitch settled gingerly on the opposite end. He suddenly found the toes on his gray socks of unquestioned interest and stared at them. Could he get through this without falling apart?

Perhaps it might be a good idea to just get it all out. Oh, in a weak moment, he'd run over the horrible events with Emma but never at any great depth. But he felt he owed that to Grady. It would be the first time in ages that he'd actually faced the real agony he'd gone through, without firmly shutting the thoughts into that little compartment in the back of his mind.

"Mitch?" Grady said.

"This isn't easy for me."

Grady scooted over to the middle of the sofa. "Don't, then, Mitch. I hereby release you from your promise. What shall we do instead? Want to go for a walk?" He started to get up.

"No," Mitch said firmly, pulling Grady back down onto the sofa. "I want to tell you. We've been so completely open with each other so far. I finally need to get this out into the light, and I think you're exactly the right person to hear my story—and now is the perfect time."

"Okay."

"I would imagine that you and Hank probably discovered your sexual attraction—love, if you will—slowly. Since you'd been together since babyhood, it couldn't have been a sudden surprise."

"Right. It seemed to dawn on him first. But when he spoke up, I realized he was right."

"Well, unlike you, I had no clue. I had a fantasy of meeting a 'Mr. Right' someday, but certainly not in my immediate future. I was so very closeted, for one thing, so the vibes I gave off were undoubtedly pseudostraight."

"Great word."

"I am a writer, you know."

"Sorry, go on."

"I took this course in creative writing—actually it was about 'Writing the Novel'—very lofty. And when I walked into the class, my first glance landed on this striking guy. Good-looking, but far from movie-star handsome. He was—the only word, although it's kind of hokey—absolutely adorable. My heart actually started beating faster. I always thought that was a myth. Tall, blond, he looked like he'd just stepped off a John Deere tractor at some farm in the Midwest. His name turned out to be Jared. Great name, right? Anyway, I was so befuddled, I didn't know quite what to do. I stumbled into the only vacant chair—naturally it was the one right next to him—and found my notebooks of great interest. I could feel my face flaming."

"How did he react?"

"I never knew until he told me much later because I didn't look up once during the entire period."

"Sounds like a profound experience."

"That it was. He told me that he'd done pretty much the same thing I did. He sat stiff as a statue and then took careful and copious notes—which he couldn't even decipher the next day."

"That's sweet."

Mitch looked up and saw that Grady understood perfectly. It was sweet. Sweeter than any candy he'd ever tasted.

"Anyway, we all had to write a scene in a proposed novel and read it in front of the class for criticism. We were allowed to ask friends or other people in the class to read with us. Jared asked me to come to his apartment to practice."

"And you said no."

"Are you kidding? I said yes so fast I didn't even think first. I don't think I spent more time getting ready for anything ever. Whether to wear this color or that shirt or those pants. Not to get too dressed up. Not to look too casual. I was frantic. When I finally got to his place and he opened the door, looking positively incredible, I stepped in and promptly dropped my books and papers on the floor while he shut the door, and then we were in each other's arms. And here comes a cliché for you—we didn't have sex. We made love. Oh, we were passionate, but it was love!"

"Oh my God," Grady whispered. "You knew."

"Right from the moment he opened the door. And we stayed in love for almost two years—and then he was gone."

"What—"

"Oh, we didn't split up or anything like that. It was an automobile accident."

"No."

"I got a phone call. A drunk driver passing over the midline of the San Francisco-Oakland Bay Bridge had collided head-on with Jared's car. It was only of limited solace when they told me that Jared had died instantly, had felt no pain."

"Oh, Mitch—" Grady began, reaching out to touch Mitch on the arm.

"Excuse me for a minute." He jumped up and hurried into the bathroom, shutting the door behind him. Glancing in the mirror, he saw his eyes fill up and spill over. He made no sound. Just the streaming of tears. He willed himself to stop it. And after a time, he didn't know how long, it was over. He wiped his eyes, blew his nose, steadied himself, splashed water on his face and dried it on a soft white towel, and then returned to the living room.

"Sorry about that."

"No need," Grady replied softly. "How tragic. What you must have gone through."

"I was pretty non compos mentis for a while. And then, as Emma noted, life went on."

"Not the same, though."

"No, especially since I also lost Pretzel."

"Pretzel?" Grady asked.

"Jared's little dachshund. He just seemed to get weaker and weaker, and I couldn't seem to do anything to save him. I think he died—I think he died of a broken heart. Pets do that, you know. He was the cutest thing. He had no hair on the end of his tail from it hitting the floor when he wagged it all the time. I got to love that little guy almost as much as I loved Jared."

"So, with such a loss, nothing's been the same for you."

"No, nothing's been the same for a long time. In some ways, I think I died with him—and little Pretzel—or at least my emotions did. I carved this safe little niche for myself, not black, but not white—sort of gray. And then you—"

"Yes?"

"Well, you made me see that we all hurt—sometimes badly—from time to time, but at least we're alive. You've already had the courage to face your troubles and try to make the best of things. You showed me quiet courage. Might be a kind of wake-up call, if I can only make myself listen. So, you see, you've paid me back in such a way that I think I actually owe you."

"Why don't we call it even," Grady said and smiled.

"All right," Mitch agreed and smiled back. There seemed to be many words unspoken between them.

Chapter Three

LATER, AS the two of them stood before Emma's door, both in sweats, as if they were going out to play volleyball, Mitch rang the bell in a little series of dots and dashes that announced who it was before she opened the door.

"Hi, guys," she said, looking even shorter in slippers. Bunny slippers!

"Bunny slippers?" Mitch asked with a laugh.

"Never mind," she snapped.

"But, Emma, bunny slippers?"

"I said, never mind."

"But, Emma, bun—"

Her fierce look shouted, "Never mind!" even louder than words.

"From Sarah, perhaps?" Mitch quipped, guessing Emma would never buy such things on her own.

"If you must know," she said gruffly as she led them into her apartment.

Grady shook his head and smiled at Mitch, who smiled back.

"Just a friend," he said to Emma.

"Just a friend. That's what I said." This through gritted teeth.

"If you say so."

"I think they look—unique, fun," Grady offered, obviously trying to remain neutral. "So, your friend has good taste in footwear as well."

Mitch resisted asking, as well as what? Instead he said, "Em, it's so nice of you to loan us your car. We need to go get Grady's clothes. He's going to stay with me for a while."

Not saying anything, she let a knowing smile possess her lips, and disappeared into her bedroom.

While Mitch was used to the décor in Emma's apartment, he saw it anew through Grady's eyes. The large windows were covered in delicate lace curtains and pull shades with satin fringes at the bottom. The huge fireplace mantel, much like Mitch's own, was covered with a long, tasseled maroon velvet runner on which stood two ornate silver candlesticks holding ivory candles, each with a bobeche at their base to catch the drips. In the center was an ormolu clock covered with an intricate flower design. Above was an ornately gilded mirror, held tilting forward slightly by heavy gold braids. Down below, on one side of the embroidered fire screen was an old-fashioned copper firewood bucket and on the other a set of fire implements. The overstuffed sofa and chair actually had antimacassars on the arms and the back. A rounded glass china cabinet held various vases and Hummel shepherds and shepherdesses, as well as several cut-crystal objects, one an ornate castle. At one side of the frieze chair stood a delicate wood smoking stand (although neither Emma nor Caroline had smoked). The Oriental rug on the floor was worn but still a rich mixture of colors—magenta, rust, ochre, and blue. A crystal chandelier hung from the ceiling, its faceted drops reflecting the afternoon sun.

"This whole place seems out of character for Emma," Grady said.

"This was all Caro's doing," Mitch told him. "Emma gave her carte blanche with the décor. She didn't really care as long as Caro was happy. Now she won't change a thing because, in a way, it feels like Caro's still here."

"Back off, Buster" came a raucous, reedy voice seemingly out of nowhere. Grady was visibly startled and stepped back a bit, but Mitch just smiled.

"That's just Tweet," he said, pointing to where a brilliantly colored green parakeet stood on a little stand in one corner.

"Hey, Mitch," it croaked. "Hey, Mitch!"

"Hi, Tweet," he replied and then said to Grady, "Caro taught him to say things."

"Just an uncaged talking green parakeet named Tweet who calls you by name? And you say that's just Tweet?" Grady said.

"He was Caro's, and she named him Tweety Bird. Emma wouldn't call him that, said he'd be embarrassed because he was a boy, so they compromised on Tweet."

"How could they tell he was a boy?"

"Well, it turns out that if that little place above a parakeet's bill that surrounds the nostrils, which is called its cere, is blue, it's a boy. If it's either tan or yellow, it's a girl."

"How do you happen to know something so arcane?"

"Emma researched it. She was determined to avoid calling any pet Tweety Bird."

Grady walked over toward the bird on its little stand.

"Careful," Mitch warned. "He's not too friendly at first. He has to get to know you. Em has to sort of introduce you to him. He wouldn't let me near him for over a month."

Grady stopped in front of the parakeet and, mumbling incoherent sounds, held out his finger. After eyeing him for several long moments, Tweet picked up one small clawed foot and placed it slowly on Grady's finger, followed after a time by the other. The two of them stared at each other for a long time. Mitch held his breath, fearing injury to one or the other.

Grady lifted the little bird up nearer his face, still mumbling the unintelligible sounds, and Tweet emitted a sort of guttural cheep. Then Tweet ducked his head against Grady's cheek.

"Well, I'll be damned," Emma said, entering the room. "He's never let a first-timer anywhere near him, much less given his august approval."

"Good judge of character," Mitch said.

As the two of them watched, Tweet very regally returned to his perch and once there hollered, "He's a keeper!"

As Grady returned, the other two roared with laughter as the little bird squawked several phrases, one being, "Hi, Mitch. He's a keeper!"

"A prophet?" Emma gasped pointedly as she recovered from the laughing fit. She held her car keys over Mitch's hand. She looked at them both with a poignant stare and said, "I assume you'll both tell me what this is all about someday."

"Promise," Grady said before Mitch could stammer out an answer. She dropped the keys into Mitch's hand.

"Deal."

"Oh no," Mitch said. "Now she's got two of us to quiz all the time and then mother-hen."

Emma cackled like a chicken, and the three of them broke up with huge guffaws. As they left, Mitch kissed her cheek. "Thanks, Em."

To his surprise, Emma lifted her check to Grady for a kiss, which he delivered without any pause. Like they were all just one big family. Nice!

As he backed carefully out of the very-rare-in-New York single-car garage under Emma's apartment, Mitch felt he should explain about the car. It was a practically mint-condition 1959 Dodge D-500 Custom Royal Lancer, painted cream and aqua with sweeping tail fins, dual antennas, red rocket-like taillights, and what looked like chrome eyebrow arches over the dual headlights. It had been Caroline's pride and joy. She'd saved up for it practically from high school, and it had been a great day for her—for them—when she'd gone out and bought it.

"With Caro gone I thought she'd want to get rid of it. Emma didn't drive. But she practically bit my head off. She would keep it, she informed me, and I would teach her how to drive. That was an interesting time period. But she did learn to drive, got her license and everything. But she doesn't really like it. The car just sits there most of the time. I take it out every once in a while, just to keep it in good order, even though I worry about dangerous drivers—it's probably worth about $50,000. But she'll never get rid of it. She told me it was Caro's favorite thing in the whole world—next to Emma and Tweet, of course. So try not to notice when people stare at us. It's in perfect condition, and you don't see many cars of this era around. People tend to stare. You get used to it."

Grady looked through the windows all around, particularly the back ones, so he could take in the sweeping fins. "I love it," he said. "Cars really had style in those days. All the cars look the same today, just a bunch of box shapes. You can hardly tell one from another."

"Except the Jeep and the Volkswagen."

"Right. If I were to have a car, it would be a Jeep Wrangler. Great lines."

"Agreed," Mitch said happily. Another thing in common?

As they drove toward the park, Mitch tried to keep his good mood intact, though he wanted at times to yell out the window at pedestrians, "Are you purposely daring me to kill you?"

At one point Grady exclaimed in surprise, "Hey, these seats swivel!"

"Em made Caro go for every possible comfort. She loved to swivel around as they drove along. Caro was always trying to calm her down. Fat chance!"

THROUGH SOME convenient bushes, they saw the volleyball players lunging and sweating, and Grady pointed Hank out to Mitch. From a distance he seemed a well-set-up kind of guy. Mitch felt a strange emotion. Could it be jealousy?

"Let's go," he whispered, even though there was no way the players could hear them. "This might be our only chance."

They hurried back to the car, jogging as they neared it, and took off.

"Which way do we go? I never asked you. Where is your condo?"

"One Morton Street."

"One Morton Street? *The* One Morton Street?"

"Yeah. Hank wanted an impressive address. And he had the money."

"Wow. Very posh! I didn't realize I was hobnobbing with high society."

"Quit it."

Mitch chuckled but couldn't help adding, "Aren't your neighbors Martha Stewart and Kevin Kline? I'd definitely call that place a celebrity hangout."

"Mitch, please," Grady said. "To tell you the truth, I never really liked it that much. Hank loved it, so I just went along. I like a place that's—well—cozier."

"Like—"

"Yeah, like yours. Homey."

Mitch was lucky in that he only had to circle the area four times before he found a parking place practically in front of Grady's building. They tumbled out of the car and through the lobby, where the doorman greeted Grady with a quick but puzzled hello at their speed. The heavily mirrored elevator seemed to take forever to reach the third floor. Grady led Mitch down the thickly carpeted hallway and into the apartment.

Mitch's immediate impression was one of starkness. The furniture was chrome and black cloth with an angular look. Some very strange modern paintings hung on the grayish walls, smears of primary colors that Mitch would have had trouble living with for very long. No rugs adorned the highly polished hardwood floors, which had an intricate inlaid pattern. Mitch found it had a very cold and forbidding feel—or was his a biased opinion?

He noticed Grady studying his face intently. "Wow, I see this room through your eyes. It's pretty austere, isn't it. I never really noticed. Hank had a decorator, and they both loved it. I was never crazy about the chrome, but I figured the decorator knew best."

"I'm sorry…."

"No need. Let's just get my stuff, and get out of here."

Mitch noticed that Grady hesitated before opening the bedroom door.

"You going to be okay?"

"I have to be. But let's make this as fast as possible. I feel like the atmosphere here is toxic."

Mitch helped Grady pull two large suitcases down from a shelf in the walk-in closet. They began filling them with Grady's clothes. A pleasant smell seemed to emanate from Grady's things. His cologne. Ahhhh. Mitch was entranced. He resisted pulling a navy blue cashmere sweater up to his nose. Soon the suitcases were full.

"I'll get some garbage bags for the rest," Grady said. He disappeared for a few moments, then returned with a couple of bags.

Shoes and workout clothes went in one bag. Socks, briefs, T-shirts, ties, and plastic-wrapped shirts in another; they were soon through. Mitch idly noticed the chrome and black with gray walls motif continued into the bedroom. Depressing!

He remembered reading somewhere that rooms should never be painted gray or lavender because both colors were depressing when used for decor.

As they returned to the living room, Mitch asked, "Isn't there something else, some knickknacks, photos, some mementoes?"

"Nothing," Grady said. "I only want my stuff. Nothing else. Nothing else means anything to me anymore. Besides, there aren't a lot of knickknacks. The decorator didn't approve of them." He took one last look around the room, sighed deeply, and turned to the door, carrying the two suitcases. Mitch followed him with the shiny black garbage bags, which felt almost slimy in his hands.

As they pulled away from the curb, the silence lasted for quite a long time.

"Are you feeling okay?" Mitch asked finally.

"Not really. I feel like I just lost a huge part of my life. It's like Hank ruined everything that went before. It's difficult to have good memories now. It all seems fake, made up. I have this feeling of groundlessness, like I'm sort of floating in some kind of limbo." He looked over at Mitch. "Don't worry, Mitch. I'll get over it. I think being back here brought this on. It'll pass. I read not long ago that the thing to do with unpleasant memories is to pile up new memories on the top until they're buried."

"Good advice," Mitch replied, feeling like a bit of a hypocrite. That's probably what he should have tried to do, instead of withdrawing into his own little emotional cave. But maybe, just maybe, it wasn't too late to venture out.

Another long silence followed.

"What are you thinking?" Mitch asked.

"I'm thinking, thank God you found me. I don't know where I'd be now if you hadn't come along. Oh, I wouldn't have jumped off a bridge or anything like that. But I sure wouldn't be where I am right now. I truly think you saved my sanity. I was right on the edge."

"Aw, Grady," Mitch muttered. He was all choked up. He cleared his throat and said, "You know the old Chinese saying that if you save someone's life, you're responsible for them forever after?"

"I wouldn't burden you with that."

"I don't think it would be a burden," he mumbled. He couldn't look at Grady. He must have been crazy to say that out loud, even in a gruff mumble.

They didn't speak further until they reached Emma's garage door and eventually parked the car inside.

Before Mitch could leave the car, Grady put his hand on his arm. "You must know, Mitch, that from this day on, I'll always be there for you."

Mitch didn't want to pull away from Grady's warm hand on his arm, but he also didn't want to give the wrong impression. He finally nodded, pointed to the doors, and left the car. They stopped at Emma's to return her keys.

"Well," she said, "that didn't take long."

"We were lucky—no trouble."

"I'm no fortune-teller but I think I see some big changes ahead."

"What's that supposed to mean," Mitch said.

"As you found it necessary to mention this morning, 'If the shoe fits'—"

"What is this," he insisted, "the day of old sayings?"

Looking down, Grady offered, "Maybe it's the day of bunny slippers?"

Emma laughed along with them. She took her keys and with an enigmatic smile closed the door. "You'll see," she said just as the lock clicked.

They went upstairs to Mitch's place and into Grady's room (that was how Mitch thought of it now) and began to put clothes into the closet and the drawers of the two chests that filled one wall. Mitch unloaded the suitcases and bags and let Grady place the items as he wanted. He felt sort of shy when handing Grady his briefs and T-shirts. When he pulled the dark blue cashmere sweater out of the suitcase, he couldn't resist pulling it quickly to his face for a hint of the enticing cologne. He looked at Grady, who had his back turned. That was stupid—what if he'd been seen?

Worse—why had he felt compelled to do it?

AS THE weeks went by, a pattern emerged. Grady would go off to work and/or an audition, and Mitch would settle down to writing. Oddly enough his writing was easier, faster, and better. He'd feared it would be just the opposite, considering he now had Grady to think about—their schedules and such, of course. And Mitch stopped going to the gym and used his Vectra with Grady as they gradually became workout partners. This was a mixed blessing for Mitch, as he couldn't help noticing Grady's sculpted muscles, prominent and glistening with sweat. Quite often he would have to think about the Four Horsemen of the Apocalypse riding toward him with annihilation in mind, or be horrendously embarrassed. He found the fear of bodily injury a great deterrent. There were times when he thought Grady might be hearing the clatter of hoofbeats in his thoughts as well.

Ah, what to do? Go back to using the gym? No, he didn't think so. He'd just have to be strong. That was it. Strong, with a great appreciation for terrifying myths.

One day Grady burst through the door late in the afternoon, shouting, "Mitch! Mitch, I got a callback. I got a callback!"

Mitch jumped up from his computer in midsentence, crossed to Grady, and took both his hands. "Congratulations. I knew you could do it. After hearing you on your monologues, I know you're really good." He realized he was still holding Grady's hands and dropped them.

"And I sang first. Usually you read first."

"What did you sing?"

"Well, they asked for a comedy song, so I did 'Artificial Flowers' from *Tenderloin*."

"I don't know it.

"Alone in the world was poor little Anne," Grady sang with great exaggeration. "It's kind of hokey, but it's supposed to be. But here's the surprise. When I finished that, they wanted to hear a ballad."

"Is that good?"

"That is terrific. They never waste their time unless they're really interested. They just say the universally dreaded, 'Thank you.' To an actor it's like a guillotine dropping." Grady tossed his briefcase on the sofa and sat down beside it.

"So what did you sing?

"I did 'All I Care about Is Love' from *Chicago*. It's probably not really a ballad, but I feel confident when I sing it for some reason, so I use it when I can. But it must have worked. I've got a callback to read for them. They'll have sides for us."

"What's a side?" Mitch asked as he picked up his scattered papers and put them back on his desk.

"It's a little booklet with just your scene in it, not the whole script."

"What musical are they doing?"

"They haven't made a final decision, but they're pretty much set on *Carousel*."

"Did they mention a specific part?"

"Yeah, Mr. Snow, you know, 'When The Children Are Asleep,' et cetera." He sang a few bars. "It's really almost a tenor role, but I do have the high note."

"You're, what, a baritone?"

"High baritone. Of course, I'd rather do Billy and get to sing the 'Soliloquy,' but they don't see me as a roustabout."

Mitch, having straightened up his desk, perched on the side, facing Grady.

"Probably the suit."

"Could be, or that I look too corn-fed."

"Right off a John Deere tractor. When's the callback?"

"Saturday at two. Two days from now."

"I'm so happy for you. You deserve a bit of good luck. We should celebrate. I know—let me take you out to dinner."

"Aw, Mitch, you've done too much already, I...."

"No. This is a big deal. I'd really like to do this."

Grady paused. Then brightened and replied, "Okay, let's do it."

As Grady was still wearing his business suit, having gone to the audition directly from work, Mitch quickly changed into slacks, a black turtleneck, and a sport coat. Then they set out, down Perry Street to Seventh Avenue, then south to Charles Street and a left, then all the way to Greenwich and then a right turn.

39

As they rounded the corner where Charles Street dead-ended at Greenwich, they passed Robert Altman's upscale furniture store, mostly white tones and very beautiful. Grady stopped to marvel at the white sofa, white figurines, white lamps, and a few turquoise objects for a splash of color. Wogies, a usually crowded sports bar that was rather trendy, took up the other corner on the left, and was, as usual, emitting noisy laughter and the clinking of glasses.

A half a block later, they were in front of Maracas, a bustling Mexican restaurant.

"Mexican?" Grady asked. "I figured we'd go to that little organic place I saw across the street."

"No. I want you to taste their guacamole. I treat myself every once in a while. Avocados are good for you. I manage to convince myself that the mayonnaise is really fat-free. Wait until you taste it. Heavenly."

They stopped at the entrance, where a wooden stand stood holding the menu, flanked on either side by outside tables protected by canvas partitions. The buzz of many conversations caused Mitch to lean in close to Grady's ear.

"You check the menu. I'll ask the hostess if we can get a quiet table inside. It usually gets pretty rowdy here—everybody's always having such a good time."

Once seated and having ordered, guacamole was served in a black molcajete bowl heavy enough to be made of steel. When Mitch passed it to Grady, it almost slipped through Grady's hands. Great surprise registered on his face at the sheer weight of it.

"What is this thing, black concrete?" Grady asked as he lowered the bowl to the tabletop very carefully.

"It's called a molcajete bowl, and it's carved from basalt. It usually has a pestle, and besides guacamole, it's used to grind herbs. It has a history dating back to the Aztec and the Mayan cultures."

"How do you know all this?"

"I set a scene in this restaurant in one of my novels, and I did some research to make it sound authentic," Mitch told him.

"And you remembered all that?"

"I have pretty good retention."

"I'll say."

And then, like a runaway train, after they finished the guacamole, they both decided to run amok gastronomically and ordered chicken burritos.

From time to time, Mitch allowed himself to order anything he felt like. That way, he never felt deprived and could also satisfy his sweet tooth with ice cream, his favorite food. He'd always said that if he could only have one food for the rest of his life, it would be ice cream.

As they were finishing their meal, suddenly lights flashed, strobes turned, and all the waiters and waitress appeared wearing sombreros, some shaking maracas and one holding a cake with sparklers in it. Using the melody of "Happy Birthday," they were singing "Congratulations to You" as they approached.

Grady blushed so red Mitch could see it in the artificial light and gasped, "You didn't."

"Who, me?" Mitch responded innocently. "I didn't do anything. I suppose they guessed. Or word travels fast." He shrugged.

When they'd finished and everything had quieted down again, Grady put his face down on his hands on the table. "I've never been so embarrassed," he muttered.

Mitch ruffled his hair and replied, "You loved it. We all love that kind of thing... even if it is excruciatingly embarrassing at the time. It's human nature."

"Alien nature, you mean. Nature from another planet." But when he looked up again, he grinned. "You are simply too much." The tone, however, seemed to say much more. Or at least it seemed so to Mitch.

As they walked back toward Mitch's apartment, Grady said, "Here we've been discussing my career at great length, and I don't even know what kind of writing you do."

"I write gay-themed novels."

"Really?"

"Yes, as you probably noticed, I read a lot of both gay and straight books. In the gay field, I got so tired of books that had sad endings. Oh, it's very seldom now that one of the main characters dies or commits suicide. Although it still happens, you don't get stuff like this too often anymore, but there was a time, not too long ago, when this was the common trend.

"Blaine and Rod stood at the ocean's edge, staring at the flaming sunset. They looked at each other for a long moment and hugged, each knowing he would never forget the other and their time together. And then Blaine walked slowly away to the north and Rod walked slowly to the south just as the sun disappeared below the horizon. The end. The bloody end. I once literally threw a book against the wall I was so disappointed and furious. Why a lot of authors of gay novels can't seem to let their characters have a happy ending puzzles me greatly. I get all caught up in the characters and I'm pulling for them, and then the author decides they should split—usually for the stupidest of reasons."

"Wow, you do get furious. I can hear it in your voice."

"Well, we haven't gotten too much beyond the time when a gay novel had to end in suicide."

"Perpetuating the myth that being gay in itself is the worst of the worst," Grady agreed. "I don't read that many novels, but I read enough to see what you mean. So I imagine you decided to do something about the situation."

"I decided to try to write what I liked to read."

"And it worked."

"Sort of. I get along. I get published enough to depend on my writing financially. But I need a wider audience."

"But you've only been at it how long?"

"Just a couple of years."

"What would it take to be immensely successful?"

"Well, a Lambda Award wouldn't hurt."

"I take it that's something like an Academy Award in movieland?"

"It's very prestigious."

"Can I read one of your stories?"

"Sure. But I don't want to put you on the spot. What if you don't like it?"

"Knowing you, even for this short time, I'm pretty sure I'll like it, probably a lot."

"We'll just have to see, won't we," Mitch said cautiously. But inside he was humming with delight. His heart and soul were in his books, and it was one way for Grady to know him in depth. This, for some reason, was important to him.

WITH A gust of warm wind smelling of the sage growing just outside the door, Grady came in after work the day of his callback.

Mitch noticed a rather perplexed look on his face. "What's wrong?" Mitch asked him.

"Well, I have the good news and—good news—and bad news."

"That statement certainly has my undivided interest."

Grady set his briefcase down and settled against one of the brown corduroy sofa pillows. Mitch dropped into the chair opposite, throwing one leg over the arm.

"They really liked me," Grady continued. "They said so right out."

"I take it that's the good news."

"Oh, yes. But they're still having more auditions upstate, up near the theater, and they can't make a final decision until they read all the local people. It's the right thing to do, and they don't want people to think they consider New York actors the only ones good enough for them. They won't make the final decision for a month or two. I don't blame them—it would be bad PR not to do that."

"But it makes for a kind of limbo? Right?"

"Right."

Grady stood, opened his shirt collar, then pulled off his tie and slipped out of his jacket and laid them neatly over the back of the sofa before sitting down again.

"But what's the other good news?" Mitch asked. "What's that all about?"

"Well, I figured out long ago that the only thing to do is keep going to auditions. If you wait on just one, and it doesn't come through, you've wasted all that time. So I got a copy of *Backstage* and found an audition for a showcase I could make if I really hurried. They're doing Shakespeare."

"That's great. Did they see a latent Hamlet?"

"God, I hope not. I hate *Hamlet*."

"Oh?" Mitch said, surprised.

"I know it's arguably his most famous and popular tragedy, but I find it a great bore. I've seen so many productions, hoping that *this time* I'll like it. But I always want to go up on stage and shake Hamlet and say, 'For God's sake, *do* something.' Four acts of waffling and in the fifth act there's bodies lying everywhere, and then Fortinbras comes in and says, more or less, 'Hi, everybody, I've come to take over.' Curtain."

Mitch couldn't help the smile that this produced. He'd fallen asleep the first time he'd seen *Hamlet*, although he'd never admitted it to anyone.

Mitch stood, saying, "Grady, you're still so tense. Relax a bit, or you'll pop. I'll get us a couple of Diet Cokes." He crossed the room, straightened an Ansel Adams cactus photo on the wall as he passed by, and disappeared into the kitchen. "Or would you rather have Crystal Light?"

"What flavor?"

"I don't remember. It's red."

"Okay" came Grady's voice. "So now I have to learn a Shakespearian monologue." Mitch heard him fumbling in his briefcase, he supposed for a play script. "Oh, and they're doing *Othello*, which is one of my favorites, and when I went in, I thought I might have a shot at Cassio. But here's the really good part—they want me to prepare one of Iago's speeches. One of the assistants, the guy who had the signup list and who was monitoring the door, told me they're thinking of playing him as a younger man, promoted to captain fast, more Cassio's age and therefore even more his competition. And, get this, some indication he lusts after Othello too."

Mitch opened the big refrigerator, feeling the sudden gust of cold air, and got out two tall cobalt glasses—he loved that amazing blue color—and placed them on the shiny stainless steel counter.

"At least that would be a different interpretation. Make him even more evil and certainly more complex, if that's possible." He poured the cold drinks and put the pitcher back in the refrigerator.

"Yes, it's puzzled many people why at the end of the play he says, 'I never shall speak more.' You'd think he'd say a lot more. And they're also thinking of setting it in the present, with the war being in Iraq."

"Won't the purists scream?" Mitch offered, entering the living room once again.

"Naturally. But it never bothers me when Shakespeare is set in a different era or has a different interpretation, as long as they don't change the speech. I saw a production where everyone spoke in the vernacular. They all sounded like Brooklyn stevedores."

Mitch laughed. "Do you think American actors should use a British accent?" He handed Grady one of the glasses and sat down on the other end of the sofa with a strong, but uneasy feeling that he needed to be closer to Grady.

"I don't like that either. It always sounds phony. I think it's best to use what they call 'elevated speech.'"

"What's that?"

"Well, my own version is to elongate the vowels a bit and make sure the consonants are crisp."

"So, can I do anything to help you learn the monologue?" He took a big swallow of his drink and immediately gave himself a headache from the coldness. He kept his face immobile, not wanting to look like a jerk. "Owww," he mumbled to himself, hoping Grady didn't hear him, "that really, really hurt!"

"Nobody can help me at first. I usually learn a script by memorizing one line and then adding the next line and so forth, until I've got the whole thing. I usually lose parts of it and have to go back and drill myself until I've got it solidly."

"Is that the way most actors do it?"

"Not really. Seems everyone has their own favorite method. In college I worked a couple of times with a guy who just read the dialogue over and over. I guess he thought he could absorb it... like osmosis."

"Did it work?"

"Not very well. It was always touch and go until opening night. Somehow, he'd always manage to get it together by then. Of course when the curtain went up, the rest of the cast was thoroughly panicked. But he was such a good actor the directors kept taking a chance until—"

"Oh no, disaster struck!"

"More or less." He laughed.

God, he looked so cute when he laughed, Mitch always had the urge to laugh along with him. He was suddenly taken aback by a fluttering in his chest. Danger!

He would not go there. He realized he was needy, but he was not going to let himself be vulnerable again. And it truly wasn't fair to Grady; he undoubtedly wasn't in the market for romance so soon after being disillusioned. He realized Grady had gone on speaking.

"We were doing a production of *Heaven Can Wait*, and one of the leading characters is a ghost. In one scene you only hear his voice because he's become invisible. My friend couldn't get through the dress rehearsal at all. He had the first scene down perfectly and then went to pieces. He apologized eighty million times, but that didn't solve much."

"What did you do, cancel?"

"No. In desperation, the other lead got the idea that he should only be a voice through the whole play and read from the script offstage."

"Brilliant."

"I thought so… since I was the other lead…. Joe the prize fighter! Survival instinct, I'm sure."

Mitch put his empty glass down on the ebony end table. He imagined Grady in boxer's trunks and nothing else and grew warm all over "So, how can I help you?"

"You could help me run my lines. I'd appreciate it. Then I'll perform it for you full-out—like a performance… if I get the part."

"I'd really like that. And, now, what's the bad news?"

"Oh, Mitch, it's more disgusting than bad. There was an actor at the callback who was a friend of mine and Hank's, when we were a couple. He and his partner and the two of us used to go out to dinner from time to time. He's an older character actor. He was auditioning for

Desdemona's father. He and his partner were kind of an inspiration to me. They've been together for almost twenty years and are still crazy about each other. I figured Hank and I would end up the same."

"So a long-term relationship can happen," Mitch said, somewhat in wonder.

"I've seen it happen. Anyway, he asked about Hank, and I told him we'd split and the reason. After hemming and hawing a while, he told me he'd wanted to tell me many times but hadn't wanted to cause trouble. Apparently, they saw Hank on several occasions picking guys up."

"Aw, no."

"So, this wasn't a one-time thing after all." Grady set his empty glass on the floor at the side of the sofa.

"Are you okay?"

"Strangely enough, at this point it didn't surprise me much. I think as far as Hank is concerned, my emotions are banked—like the ashes of a dead campfire," he intoned dramatically. "I was more startled than upset. How could I have been so stupid?"

Mitch slid over the sofa and put a hand on Grady's shoulder. "You weren't stupid, Grady. You were trusting. You thought that Hank was just like you, honest and straightforward. You, my friend, are not like other people. You're a special breed."

Grady leaned forward and put his elbows on his knees. Mitch's hand slipped away, and it felt almost as cold as the headache he'd just suffered.

"Grady, just don't let this make you cynical. Don't let this one thing change you."

Grady got up and, in long strides, crossed to the window and looked out. "I don't think I could change even if I wanted to. I'm just me. I think I'll always be just me."

"Good," Mitch replied. "Me" was absolutely splendid.

"GRADY," MITCH asked, "would it be all right with you if I went to your callback for *Othello* with you? I've got an idea to make my next lead character an actor, and I'll need to know all the specifics."

Mitch was sitting at his desk. He'd been having a very productive morning, attacking the keyboard ferociously as the words came into his head faster than he could type... and he was a very, very fast typist. He wondered if it was because Grady was sitting across the room, studying his script, preparing for the callback. The atmosphere was so... what... comfortable? Homelike? Mitch couldn't actually put his finger on the exact cause, but he realized it had something to do with Grady's presence. Grady looked up and smiled.

"Sure, Mitch. I'd actually feel better if I knew you were there. Moral support, you know. They probably won't let you come into the actual audition with me, but you could soak up the atmosphere, all the hideous nervous tension in the room where all the actors are waiting for a chance to do their bit."

"Is it really that bad?"

"Worse. I know a guy who was an assistant director, and he told me that once they were casting six parts and they got—hang on to this—about a hundred photos and résumés for each part!"

"Wow!"

"Actors are desperate to perform, and the chances of being cast are so slim as to be almost nonexistent. The percentages are almost as bad as winning the lottery."

"And I've heard," Mitch put in, "that your chances of winning the lottery are less than that of being hit by lightning. Twice. In the same place!"

Suddenly Mitch was aware of heavy rain hitting the big window across the room from his desk. He got up and went to sit on the other end of the sofa, opposite Grady. He looked at his friend for a long moment and thought how pleasant it was to sit here in the warm room, with the pelting rain tattooing the window, and enjoy the closeness with this great guy. As thoughts of danger entered his head, typical when he let himself think warm thoughts about Grady, he pushed them aside with some effort and decided to simply enjoy the moment. The darkened sky left the room dimmer than it had been with only his desk lamp and the Tiffany lamp beside the sofa casting a soft glow. Yes, he liked this atmosphere very much. He realized that he heard Grady's voice cut through his musings.

"I think most actors would rather get a good agent than win the lottery." He paused a moment before going on. "Of course, if you won the lottery, you could produce and star in your own show, so I guess that would be the better choice."

"Oh, I understand. It's almost as hard for a writer to get a literary agent. I know. I've tried. What they really want is for you to be successful on your own, and then they want to represent you."

"Same for actors. Get a good part on your own, which, of course, is almost impossible, and they all want you. But I knew a guy who walked into an agent's office and the agent took one look and said, 'I'm signing you. I just lost an actor who looks exactly like you.' A week later he had a running part on a soap. He and his girlfriend moved from a small, dingy apartment on the West Side to a swanky joint on the East Side. Then within the month they got married and fans even turned up at the church. Everything changed that fast. But that's rarer than rare."

So it was that Mitch found himself holding on to the central bar opposite the doors on the number 3 subway, with Grady's hands just above his own. The usual crowd of passengers had plunged into the car at the Twelfth Street end of the Fourteenth Street stop as if the frantic race for a seat were a life or death matter. Old people, pregnant women, nuns—forget it—got to get that seat! As usual, Mitch waited until the mad rush, the pushing and shoving, was over and then stepped into the car, pulling Grady with him just before the chimes sounded melodically, but finally, as the doors closed. Thus, they were standing, holding on to the pole.

"So you wait for the madding crowd to explode into the car just like I do." Grady whispered into Mitch's ear just loud enough to be heard over the rumbling noises.

"You too? I couldn't stand being one of those people who becomes a killer when the subway doors open." Just then one of Grady's hands slid down the pole until it touched Mitch's hand. The tingle sent jolts all through him. He knew he should lower his own hands, but, somehow, they wouldn't move. And Grady didn't seem inclined to move his either. Warm fingers touched warm fingers, causing more sensations than such a touch would normally do. So they rode all the way to Forty-Second Street, even through the one stop at Thirty-Fourth (Penn Station), looking anywhere but at each other. When it came time to leave the car, neither spoke for a long time. After coming up out of the subway into the brightness and dazzling movement of lights that was now Forty-Second Street, Mitch finally asked which way to go.

"I'm afraid it's almost to the water on Forty-Third... a space that's soon to be up for demolition. More high-rise apartments, I guess."

So they walked side by side past the Port Authority on their left and the huge Duane Reade drugstore on the right, hardly noticing the crowds they dodged every so often. The honking of horns and the rumbling of many voices, as well as the virtual sea of yellow cabs, went unnoticed. Once, when they were separated by a rushing wedge of humanity, Mitch felt the side of him nearest Grady grow rather cold. However the atmosphere remained the same. Strange? No, maybe not so strange at all!

Finally, Mitch noticed a bunch of what undoubtedly had to be actors gathered in front of a dilapidated building, devouring what looked like scripts. This must be it. Sure enough, Grady headed across the street, and after nodding to a couple of people, led Mitch into the building. It was rather dark, musty smelling, and with dirty floors and walls that had once held wallpaper. Now it was simply curled scraps here and there. Actors seemed to be everywhere, some holding scripts in shaking hands. Poor things, Mitch mused. Eventually, they reached a large table, behind which sat a reed-thin older man who seemed to be in charge.

"Name?" he asked Mitch.

"Ah, I'm just here with my friend," he replied, indicating Grady.

"Gilmore," Grady said.

The man ran a bony finger down a smudged list of names until he found what he was looking for. "Iago," he said without looking up and selected a sheet of paper, which he held out toward Grady. The door behind the desk opened, and a scowling actor strode by, letting the door slam shut behind him. In the same monotone, the man behind the desk added, "They want to see you right away, as soon as you're ready."

"I'm ready now," Grady said evenly.

Mitch was surprised at how calm and assured Grady sounded. He felt the sense of raw nerves filling the room, just as Grady had described. The man looked up now with a rather bloodshot gaze and said, "Hmmm." He got up, ambled up to the door, and knocked softly. When a young woman came out, he peeked in and said, "Gilmore's here."

Returning to his seat, he muttered, "Go on in."

"Knock 'em dead," Mitch said, squeezing Grady's arm. He knew from former conversations never to say, "Good luck," as, perversely, that would certainly bring about bad luck. Actors seemed to be overly superstitious, but Mitch wasn't about to tempt fate either.

Mitch couldn't stand the squalid surroundings or the nervous energy, so he stepped outside into the fresh air. This close to the water, he inhaled the salty smell, which rid him of the less pleasant odors of the room he'd just left. He found himself very nervous for Grady. He wanted him to get this part almost as much as Grady wanted it for himself; he deserved some good luck right about now.

He found himself walking up and down a distance away from the crowd around the door, lost in his thoughts. So he was mildly startled to feel a firm hand on his shoulder. He turned to see a radiant Grady smiling at him.

"I got it!" Grady said, hugging Mitch to him. Mitch held him tightly for a long moment and then stepped back. Still holding Grady by the shoulders, he shook his head.

"I never doubted it for a minute… well, maybe for a minute, but that was all. Ah, Grady, I'm so happy for you!"

Comfortable, arm in arm, they started back to the subway.

Grady recited the first line of one of Iago's monologues amicably. "And what's he then that says I play the villain…."

Chapter Four

MITCH HUNG up the phone and ran his hands through his hair in mild frustration. Brandon had had that effect on him over the past few years. Best friends since kindergarten, Brandon and he had been inseparable for much of their growing-up years, until Brandon's family moved when he was sixteen. They kept in touch by phone, but in the last couple of years, Brandon had changed, actually transformed, into a totally different person. And, in Mitch's opinion, not a very nice one. And now he was coming to New York on one of his rare visits. Thank heavens he only intended to stay for a weekend. Mitch didn't know if he could stand much more than that without literally throwing him out into the street. And now there was the unpleasant task of telling Grady they were going to have obnoxious company. But how could he turn such an old friend away?

He was trying to figure out the best way to broach the subject as he sat at his computer, attempting to finish the chapter he'd been working on all day for his new book. He'd always found this little corner, with its floor-to-ceiling bookcases and the old oak rolltop desk he'd discovered at a country sale, a safe haven. But he felt unsettled as he worried the subject of Brandon around in his mind, like a stray wind might worry a fallen leaf, first this way and then that. His writing had come to a complete stop several times. And this was a key scene where the two guys realize their feelings went deeper than just liking each other's company.

Like he was with Grady—Careful there! Perhaps he was just mistaking sympathy for another emotion. That was probably it.

Now his writing was really on hold, so he stood and stretched his hands, trying to touch the ceiling, until his back realigned itself with a rather loud crack. He strode into the kitchen for a drink. When he looked in the refrigerator for the Crystal Light, he found the pitcher almost empty. He reached up into the cabinets above the drainboard, shielding his eyes from the reflection of the sun on the stainless steel sink, and found the familiar cylinder of his favorite drink. He took out one of the four little plastic containers, pulled the foil aside, and emptied the dull magenta powder into the pitcher. He let the water in the sink run hot before putting the pitcher under it for a few seconds. He loved how the powder turned bright red and the sweet fragrance floated up around him. He swirled it around until he was sure it had all dissolved and then he filled the rest of the pitcher with cold water. He couldn't wait for it to get icy, so he poured a glass and downed it lukewarm. "Mmm," he murmured, "just what I needed."

Just as he emptied the glass, he heard the front door open and then close. Grady was home. Could he help the extremely pleasant feelings that ran through him? No, but he could ignore them. Couldn't he?

"Mitch," he heard Grady call out. "Are you here?"

"Yeah, in the kitchen," he answered leaning back against the sink. "But I should be immersed in chapter ten of my book."

"Writer's block?" Grady asked as he entered the kitchen, unbuttoning his shirt collar and loosening his tie, as was his habit.

"Not really. Just writer's lack of concentration."

"Something's wrong." Grady sat down at the old oak table that had belonged to Mitch's grandmother. He toed off his loafers.

"Just a little something. I'll explain."

Mitch wished he wouldn't always zero in on those dark hairs peeking through Grady's open shirt. Ah, well….

Knowing Grady would be ravenous after work, as usual, and after pouring them both a glass of that wonderful red fluid they both loved so much, Mitch started building two gigantic turkey sandwiches. He got out the sliced turkey, tomatoes, baby spinach (instead of lettuce), low-fat mayonnaise, and two large pita pockets. He worked with the precision of an architect building a scale model.

When he'd settled at the table and they'd bitten into the juicy sandwiches, Mitch said, "My oldest friend, Brandon, is coming to visit for a weekend."

"Oh, do you need my room? I could—"

"No way. Your room is just that: your room. He can either sleep on the couch or go to a hotel."

"But, Mitch…."

"No arguments. I'm not displacing you for that crazy twit."

"Not the friend that's kept hidden in the attic, I hope?"

"Not quite. But that decision is debatable, in my opinion."

Grady laughed, then tipped his glass up to finish and got up for a refill. Mitch couldn't help noticing how smoothly Grady moved. Liquid. He was reminded of Olympic gymnasts or champion divers.

"I've been meaning to bring this up, Mitch," Grady said, leaning back against the refrigerator after filling his glass. "I seem to be— what—lingering on here in your place…."

"Have I complained? I like having you here."

"But if I mean to stay on a while, I have to start helping with the rent, et cetera."

"I've never really thought about it. Actually, it seems kind of like you've always been here. You don't need to worry about the rent or the et cetera."

"I don't want to be a freeloader."

"That's the last thing I'd think about you."

"It'll make me feel better. After all, I have a job. I'm solvent. Please, Mitch, you've got to let me help."

"Okay, okay, if it'll make you feel better."

"Good, it will. So, what's wrong with your friend?" Grady asked as he returned to the table and sat down again.

"It's a long and kind of boring story."

"Bore me."

"Okay, you asked for it. We were such good friends growing up. And my first tentative sex experience, such as it was, was with him. He was very ticklish, and I wasn't at all. He bet me there was one place I was ticklish. I said, 'Where?' Looking back, I realize he planned this carefully, because without a word he pointed to my crotch. I told him no way. He dared me. I thought my honor was at stake, as kids do when dared, so I dropped my pants and briefs, and he tickled me. Well, in about two seconds I was hard, and he wasn't tickling, he was stroking, and it felt good, so I shut up. He unfastened his own pants, and he was as hard as I was, and he put my hand on it. So in about a second and a half, we both climaxed."

"Trust me, this isn't boring," Grady said.

"Be good. This was a minor trauma." Mitch tipped his chair back on its back legs. "I knew vaguely that only 'those guys' liked that sort of thing, but, of course, once discovered, it was difficult to turn back. So whenever he'd visit, we'd indulge. Then, about a year later, his folks moved away. We talked on the phone and more or less came out to each other eventually."

"So far this sounds rather innocuous."

"I suppose so. But then he decided to come out to his parents."

"Mistake?"

"They've always been very uptight people. Apparently they freaked out and sent him to some goofy farm where they 'fix' guys who have 'misguided themselves.'"

"Oh, no."

"We all know that reparative therapy nonsense still goes on."

"And causes all kinds of unhappiness and even suicide!"

"Right." Mitch let his chair fall back on four legs with a loud thump. "Like that guy—Socarides, I think—the well-known psychiatrist who insisted it's possible to change sexual orientation. He died a while back."

"Isn't he the same guy whose son is gay?"

"That's the one."

"He should have seen a therapist. He was apparently in great denial."

They both got a good laugh out of that.

"The son, Richard Socarides, was a special assistant concerning gay issues to Clinton during his presidency."

"I wonder how he figured he could cure people of their 'bad choice' when he couldn't even change his son. Anyway," Mitch went on, "Brandon bought into this stuff and claims he's now straight and belongs to some ex-gay club or something."

"Poor guy."

"I'd agree, but he's always trying to convince me to go the same route."

"Oh, my God."

"Right. And that's probably why he's coming to visit. One more try to change the misguided sinner."

"How are you going to explain me?"

"Oh, he'll probably be very vocal about your presence."

"You could always shock him into leaving by saying we're lovers."

"R-r-right." He paused. "Good idea." Mitch's ribs suddenly felt like they just might be on the outside of his body. His mind suddenly a Kansas tornado, the idea of Grady being his lover reminded him of the time when, as a child, he'd innocently stuck his finger in a light socket and been thrown across the room. And yet, what was that pleasant sensation that seemed to take over once the surprise passed? It started at his toes and spread quickly to the top of his head, much like a window shade being raised slowly to reveal the sun.

Mitch noticed Grady looking at him strangely. Did his shock show on his face? Did Grady think he was unhappy with the idea? Did Grady wish he'd never suggested it? Did Mitch wish that? *No*, he thought to himself, *I definitely do not!* Oh God, what was he thinking?

He stood abruptly and said, "I'd better get back to my writing. I've got to finish that chapter." He quickly left the room. Really, a narrow escape!

"GUESS WHO showed up at my office?" Grady said in a muffled tone as he entered the living room while pulling a light blue sweater over his head.

"Not Hank."

"Yes."

Grady plunked himself down on the sofa.

"What happened?" Mitch's fingers grew still on his keyboard, and he stood and walked over to sit beside Grady.

"Right outside the office," Grady said, "in the hall, he started begging me to come back. That he'd made a terrible mistake. Couldn't I forgive him? Think of all we've been to each other. How long we were together."

"What did you say to him?"

"I told him no. How could I ever trust him again? That if he had it in him to bring some guy into our home, our very bed, he couldn't truly respect me very much or our relationship."

"What a horrible scene." Mitch pulled one knee up on the sofa and turned sideways to Grady while giving him a little consoling pat on his shoulder.

"It got worse. When I said I didn't want to listen to him and to get out of my way, he started yelling. How cold I was. How cruel. How unforgiving. You can imagine. I asked him how many times before that he'd cheated on me."

"And he said what?"

"He actually played innocent and asked me what I meant by that."

"You told him?" Mitch found that his hand had mysteriously returned to sit on Grady's shoulder.

"Yes. I told him I'd heard that from people who'd seen him. He worked up a few crocodile tears and said they all meant nothing to him. That I was his only love."

"Were you swayed, even a little bit?"

"That's what surprised me. Not a bit. I just wanted to get away from him. I told him to leave me alone, that I was through with him. So he pulled this almost slumping to the floor business. He used to win our disagreements by seeming to fall apart. This time I finally saw how manipulative he was."

"You have a new point of view."

"Exactly. So while he was practically on the floor, I took off down the stairs, lucked out with a cab at the front of the building, and here I am."

"He'll try again, you know." Mitch pulled his hand away from Grady's shoulder as his emotion changed from consolation to yearning. Consolation was fine; yearning was not.

"Of course he will. That's what really bothers me. He's going to stalk me."

Grady stood and walked over to the mantel. He gazed for a time at the Murano bowl, as if it had the answers to how to avoid Hank. He turned back to Mitch. "Looking back, I realize that he hangs on like a pit bull until he gets what he wants. Once, when we couldn't agree on where to go on a vacation, he was relentless. I finally agreed with him just to stop the constant arguments. I think his ego's involved more than his feelings."

They were both silent for a time.

"There's more," Grady said.

"More than that?"

"Yeah, perfect timing. There's a guy I'm sort of friendly with who temps at our place every so often. I saw him just this morning, and he asked how Hank was. I told him we'd split up—not the details, just that we were no longer a couple.

"I'll bet he was surprised."

"Not really. He hemmed and hawed a bit, and then told me the same things that my actor friend told me."

"So it was a pattern."

"Apparently. That's what gave me the guts to turn him down without a qualm. What a dunce I've been."

"As I mentioned before, you just think everyone's like you, with high standards. But they're not. I think most people are pretty self-centered. Only a few have empathy. You know, are capable of walking a mile in the other guy's boots."

Grady looked straight into Mitch's eyes and said seriously, "There's you, Mitch."

Mitch could feel himself blushing hotly. He never blushed—praise from Grady could do this?

Hmmmm.

WHEN GRADY came home from the first read-through, he was obviously flying high—a wide grin on his face and a light swing in his arms gave him away as he entered the room.

"Guess what?"

"What?"

"This is a great cast. Our Othello is about the tallest guy I've ever seen, very majestic, and a great actor. My older friend got Desdemona's father and—here's the great news—my dear friend Patty Ingram is going to play Emilia. We've done several shows together. I thought she was on the road with a tour, but she got back just a week ago and read for this play. She was going to call me but thought she'd wait to see if she got cast so she'd have good news. We had quite an emotional reunion in front of everyone, but I didn't care."

"You deserve some decent breaks. I'd imagine having a friend in the cast helps a lot, especially one who plays your wife."

"Yeah, from the read-through, I think it's going to be a really good show. There's only one drawback as far as I'm concerned."

"Oh? What's that?"

"The guy playing Cassio. His name is Randall Templeton III, believe it or not, and he actually puts the whole thing in his bio in a program. And if you dare call him Randy, he corrects you immediately with a kind of snotty tone. Anyway, he's wooden, as usual. But he's quite handsome, which is probably why he got the part. What's so off-putting is he knows he's great-looking, and he's arrogant about it. We've both worked with him before—me once and Patty twice. Patty told me she'd tell me some really gruesome truths about him later. Apparently she knows something about him that I don't. And I thought I knew it all."

"Ah, intrigue offstage as well as on."

"Yeah. He sort of came on to me in the other play we did together, and even after I told him I was already committed, he didn't stop. Hank used to come to rehearsals so he could give me his sage advice about my part later on. So, naturally, I complained about Randall, and one night I noticed Hank having a serious conversation with him. After that he left me alone. It was quite a relief. I asked Hank what he'd said, but he wouldn't tell me exactly. Just sort of smiled and mumbled something about being the persuasive type."

"So old Hank was good for something, at least."

"Yeah. But you'd never know anything like that had happened. Randall was almost too nice to me. Today he managed to sit next to me during the reading, and he kept touching me while we read. I had to remind him all over again that I was committed. He said, 'I thought that was all over.' So I told him it was, but that I was still committed, just not to Hank. He said, 'That was quick work.'"

"Good thing," Mitch said softly, "or I might have to have a little conversation with him myself."

"Well, I am committed—to—to my work."

"R-Right," Mitch managed finally and left the room. He suddenly felt the need to lie down. Why did he feel dizzy?

IN THE week that followed, it seemed to Mitch that time was almost floating on by, much like a pleasant summer breeze. He would hear Grady run through his lines most every night, and he even read *Othello* again in order to be acutely familiar with the entire play. In his mind he could see Grady in the part, as the assistant had described it to him. But he couldn't imagine Grady being able to portray such an evil character, even though he was undoubtedly a good actor. When they were going over Grady's lines, he always acted the part as best he could, depending on his memorization, so Mitch saw the beginnings of the evil part of the character.

"My first drama teacher told me that a good actor always does his part full-out, as best he can at the time. He never coasts, whether it's a full performance or the hundredth rehearsal," Grady told him. "So that's what I do. It's difficult to get it up to full steam until I know the piece totally. But I always do the best I can."

"The best you can do is pretty good, in my estimation," Mitch replied. "You sure scare me."

"I just wish I was a fast study."

"What do you mean?"

"A fast study, and there are very few, can read that speech for about a half an hour and then deliver it perfectly."

"No kidding."

"I've known two. Of course, I wanted to strangle both of them. They made it seem so easy, I felt like a dolt in comparison. We were doing Oscar Wilde's *An Ideal Husband*, and the actress playing Mrs. Cheveley, which is a huge part, had to drop out three days before opening. This girl named Judy Ruse stepped in and learned the part in two days, and she performed it flawlessly on opening night. Was I ever impressed."

"What are you, then?" Mitch asked.

"I guess I'd call myself a medium study. I'm fairly fast, but no way could I memorize some huge part like that in two days. I wish I could. It's a great thing to put on your résumé. Directors seem to feel you're going to be very easy to work with."

"Does that always follow?"

"No. You can be a quick study and also be temperamental. Bad combo."

"And you are…?"

"Medium study and nontemperamental. But you can't put that on your résumé. I think it makes you sound smug. I knew an actor once who put 'easy to get along with' on his résumé, but he was the most stubborn person I ever worked with, always arguing with the director about interpretation and staging. That same old teacher taught me that an actor can do anything a director asks of him. Without bragging too much, I could go over to a corner of the set, stand on my head, and make it look natural if a director told me to. He taught me that's an actor's pride—you direct me, and I can do it. At least, that's what he always claimed."

"Okay, go over in the corner and stand on your head for me."

"You are so mean. This isn't a play."

"Kidding."

"I know." But Mitch watched, fascinated, as Grady went over to a corner and stood on his head. Then he fell into a tumble and ended up on one knee with outstretched hands.

"Ta-da!" he said.

Mitch broke up laughing and applauded loudly. "I don't think you'll find that useful when you're playing Iago."

"Who knows?"

"Back to work," Mitch said seriously. "This is the middle speech, isn't it? How are you going to play it?"

"Well, they told me they want to see my interpretation without direction. So I'm going to do the first part as a very reasonable man. And then when he says, 'Divinity—of hell' I'm going to let the audience see the madness behind his congenial façade. Let them see how he fools Othello."

"I can see you forming that approach already."

"I'm going to start the speech sitting on the floor and rather casually. Almost bewildered. I took some coaching once with a very good lady who told me that the way to get attention in an audition, or even a performance, is to make some gesture before you speak. She said people will always look at action before they listen to words. And once you've got their attention, it's easier to keep it."

"Hmmm. I never thought of that."

"So I'm just going to sit there, leaning on one arm and looking at the ground, and then I'll suddenly look up, like I just noticed people are listening to me. Wave my other hand a few times, and then start."

"When do you think you'll be ready to do this full-out? I can hardly wait."

Mitch watched Grady sit on the floor and perform the actions he'd described. When he looked up, Mitch was riveted. There was a rather long pause, and then Grady began to speak.

"And what's he then that says I play the villain...."

How could sweet Grady play a villain? *Sweet Grady?* What was he thinking?

And then Grady went on into the speech. He seemed quite reasonable and sincere, but the character had already revealed his duplicitous nature. And yet he seemed so calm, so rational, it was difficult to disbelieve him. As he went on, he gave the impression of being rather kind. And then he came to the line he'd described as a transition point—'Divinity' was delivered in the same soft voice and then, rearing up on one knee, much like a cobra, he growled, '—of hell! When devils will the blackest sins put on, they do suggest at first with heavenly shows, as I do now....'" And he suddenly became a madman, spitting vitriol. The change was so sudden as to be startling. Mitch felt the need to lean away from the character as he went on and on, spitting out his despicable plans until he came to a mad crescendo at the end of the speech.

"So will I turn her virtue into pitch, and out of her own goodness make the net that shall enmesh them all!"

Mitch sat in stunned silence for a moment as pure evil disappeared and warmhearted Grady returned. "My God!" Mitch finally said, almost gasping. "That was positively scary. You seemed to disappear, and this other entity materialized. I actually wanted to get away from you!"

Grady returned a huge smile. "You couldn't have said anything that would make me happier. I really came off as the bad guy?"

"Bad isn't even the right word for this guy. He's way beyond bad."

"I love hearing that. Often, if Iago's played wrong, he's so clever he becomes charming to the audience, and that throws the whole play off-kilter. It makes Othello seem like a big dolt instead of a tragic figure. I want to make sure the audience knows who the antagonist is."

"Well, you certainly succeeded." Grady stood up, and Mitch crossed over to him and gave him a big hug. "You're really, really good, Grady," he whispered. Then, after a time, it struck him that he was still hugging his friend, reluctant to let go. Grady had put his arms around him and held on tight. Mitch thrilled at the hard muscles of Grady's back and began to be aroused. He pulled away with a quick pat on Grady's shoulders. "Buddy," he said, "you're headed for stardom." Mitch noticed a strange look on Grady's face. Was it confusion? Could it be disappointment? Mitch turned and went into the kitchen.

"This calls for a round of protein drink, in lieu of champagne," he called out. He seemed a bit short of breath. But who wouldn't be after such a stunning performance?

LATER EM'S special ring (causing the little melody to sound twice, plus the knocks) brought Mitch scrambling up and away from his desk; Em, always impatient, hated to wait.

When Mitch opened the door, that lady rushed forward in high dudgeon, her red wig slightly askew.

63

"What's wrong?" Grady asked her.

"Sit back down, boys. Have I got a tale to tell."

When they were all settled she began. "There was some guy here this afternoon asking me if I had a tenant named Grady."

"Hank," Grady said.

"Dammit," Mitch offered.

"I asked him why he wanted to know. He says that he was driving by and saw a friend enter one of these apartment houses, and he was hoping to find out which one so he could stop by and see him."

"I'll see him right back out into the street," Mitch said.

"What did you tell him?" Grady asked.

Emma leaned forward, dwarfed by the big chair she sat in, and stared at the two men on the sofa. "I told him Grady was an unusual name, that I would certainly know if I had a tenant by that name, and that I didn't."

"Fibbing, Emma?" Mitch asked.

"Not at all. I don't have a tenant named Grady. You have a guest named Grady. That's not the same thing at all."

"Good reasoning," Grady told her.

She smiled at them both. "So he said that maybe he was mistaken and that he'd seen his supposed friend going into one of the apartment houses on either side of mine. I told him that I was dear friends with the supers of both places—which I am, no fibbing there—and that I was sure they would have mentioned a new tenant named Grady. But they hadn't."

"He asked me why I assumed it was a new tenant. What a suspicious type—he must judge everybody by himself. So I told him we always discuss new tenants, if they're going to be good tenants or trouble, and no one mentioned that name either recently or in the past."

"Did he accept that?" Mitch asked.

"I think he did," she replied. "But I think he'll keep looking until he finds you, Grady."

"I'm sure you're right. But I'd like to put that off for as long as I can."

"What's your trouble with this guy?" Emma asked.

An uncomfortable silence followed.

"Curiosity killed the cat," Mitch finally said.

"I'm not a cat, and I'm not curious, just concerned." Mitch saw the concern on her face. Emma, he knew, tended toward caretaking, whether the subject wanted it or not. It was an endearing but sometimes troublesome trait. He sighed deeply.

Grady took over to settle the matter. He and Emma had bonded nicely, Mitch had noticed.

"Same sad old story," Grady said in a monotone. "He and I were partners for almost twelve years—since we were kids, actually—and I came home one day to find him cheating on me. End of story. Except that Mitch here saved me from going crazy."

"Oh," Emma said. She rose quickly and moved over beside Grady and took his hand in hers. "I'm so sorry, dear. That must have hurt terribly. But I can see you're in good hands now. Mitch would never, never betray a trust."

Mitch quickly put in, "Grady is just staying here until he can get himself together and move on."

Emma looked over at Mitch and then up into Grady's eyes.

"Yes," Grady said softly. "Sort of a way station on the way to stability."

Emma startled them both by standing abruptly and stamping her foot. "You young fools, I see what I see, and you'd better wake up before you make a horrid mistake!" she said and marched to the door and out, slamming it on the way.

Mitch and Grady had both stood when Emma stamped her foot.

"What was that all about?" Grady asked.

"Emma is a dear person, but she's very emotional and never afraid to voice her opinions. Sometimes she can be so enigmatic that you haven't the slightest inkling what she's talking about. She often comes across as Cassandra in the Greek tragedy. Usually, in time, you can figure it all out. But this one is a doozy," he added.

They looked at each other. Mitch looked away first. He'd known Emma longer. He was better at figuring her out.

Chapter Five

THEN CAME the phone call.

It had been raining all morning. When the rain wasn't splatting against the windows, it was dropping from one rung of the fire escape to the next with little melodic pings. Mitch had always found these noises very comforting, especially when either curled up in bed or tucked into the chair at his desk. Rain always seemed to promote his best writing.

He remembered as a youngster how he'd loved lying in bed, particularly when it rained like this, and fantasizing about he and Flash Gordon being best friends. Or sometimes it was Batman and he was Robin. There was undoubtedly a clue here of what was to come, but at the time he was unaware of any sexual connections. He just wanted to be a superhero's best friend. Superman, Prince Valiant, Red Ryder, Captain Marvel—any and all of them. They were his dream buddies. There was, of course, affection involved, as they would sit on a grassy slope and talk about things. What things? It never seemed important. They never went after criminals; they just sat on this grassy hill and talked. He couldn't even remember the conversations. But whenever he spun these scenarios he felt warm all over and worthy. He counted! Suddenly, like a giant rock falling into a quiet pool, the thought plowed into his mind that this scene was exactly what had happened with Grady. Even the strange feeling of warmth was similar.

He remembered the very first time this sort of thing happened in real life. He was in the sixth grade, and a new kid had come into the class. Bobby Cortland. He seemed older and more worldly than Mitch and his other classmates. Everyone, boys and girls, gravitated toward him. A bunch of the guys in the class, including Mitch, used to go with him on his paper route, just to be in his company. They were all vying to be his best friend. Although he'd never put it together at the time, the feelings he'd had when in Bobby's company were similar to the way he'd felt with Flash Gordon and the others in his daydreams. How naïve he'd been in the sixth grade! Now, looking back, it seemed inevitable the way his sexual orientation played out.

But at the end of the term, actually the end of grammar school itself, as the next stage was junior high at a completely different school, Bobby Cortland had vanished from his life. Bobby's parents had moved back to Yuba City in Northern California. Mitch remembered the horrible, wrenching separation. He'd hidden in his bedroom and let the tears take over. He'd felt embarrassed being so weak, but it had truly felt like his life just might end.

Of course it didn't. Then, in his second semester in junior high, there'd been Jim Drew. Jim: very blond; baseball player; good-looking in spite of the thick glasses he had to wear. The attraction had sneaked up on him. They happened to sit next to each other in opposite rows in English class. They began to exchange words before class and then after class, and eventually Mitch asked him if he'd be interested in taking in a movie over the weekend. This became an almost weekly event. Then had come the time when, in the middle of a movie, somehow—Mitch was never sure of the sequence of events—their hands had come together down between the seats. Mitch remembered thinking that Jim didn't really realize what had happened, and that if he moved the slightest bit, Jim's hand would fly away. And he remembered desperately not wanting that to happen. His hand had gone totally asleep, but he never moved it—and then the movie was over and they were walking up the aisle. Neither ever mentioned what had happened and, disappointingly, it never happened again. However, another time Mitch had felt emboldened enough to lay his arm across the back of both Jim's seat and the empty one on his other side. Then he'd slipped his arm down to rest across Jim's shoulders. He never asked Mitch to remove it. Several times he waited, hoping Jim might return the gesture, but he never had, or at least Mitch could never wait very long before he moved his own arms. Looking back years later, Mitch realized that Jim was probably also gay and afraid to admit it. But Jim vanished from his life just like Bobby had when Jim's family moved to Redwood City for high school. Again, he was devastated. So even long before Jared, Mitch had suffered rather traumatic loss. And he'd been just a kid. He realized at some deeper level that he couldn't blame himself for his fear of loss, but he had never been consciously aware that it was not only his loss of Jared that held him captive to his fears.

That was when the ringing of the phone had interrupted his thoughts. Mitch picked up the phone, listened for a bit, and then put his hand over the earpiece. "Grady," he called from his desk in the corner of the living room, "it's for you."

Puzzled, Grady came from the kitchen, carrying a handful of silverware. He took the phone.

Mitch heard only Grady's side of the dialogue with long pauses in between.

"This is Grady. ... Really." He dropped the silverware to the top of the phone stand with a loud clatter. "When do you need me?" Mitch watched Grady's delighted expression change to disappointment. "I'm in a showcase production of *Othello*, and our closing night is a week after that date." There was a long pause. "Oh, I understand. ... Excuse me, what did you say? You think that might be possible? That would be great. You'll get back to me then. ... Okay. And thanks again, whichever way it goes, for thinking of me."

Mitch watched Grady stand there in a dreamlike trance with a crooked smile on his face.

"Well?" he asked.

Grady shook his head and came back to the real world. "It was the producers of the musical. I got it. They want me to play Mr. Snow in *Carousel*. But the rehearsals start a week before *Othello* closes."

"Oh, no. What horrible timing."

"Exactly. But I couldn't just wait to hear from them. And I've loved being in this production. I'm so proud of the cast and the director and what we've put together. I wouldn't have missed it, even for Mr. Snow."

"But just a week. You should have had them both."

"Don't I wish, I...."

The phone rang again. Mitch picked it up, listened for a moment, smiled at the words he heard, and once again said, "It's for you, Grady."

Mitch watched Grady's expression change from disappointment to delight.

"Really?" he said. There was a long pause, during which Mitch moved to the edge of his chair. Then Grady resumed. "Of course. I know I can. … Right. And—oh, God, thank you!"

He replaced the phone with a dazed look.

"They're going to send me the script and the music, and if I learn the whole part before I get there, they'll let me be a week late!"

"Oh, Grady, that's terrific," Mitch said. He practically jumped over his desk as papers floated to the floor like petals from a giant Chinese magnolia. He took hold of Grady by the shoulders and swung him in circle after circle in a weird triumphant dance. Round and round and round until they were both dizzy. They finally fell to the sofa, Mitch half off on the floor, both out of breath and laughing almost hysterically. Then Grady stopped laughing suddenly, as if a light switch had been turned off.

"I also have to be in an original show in their one-act festival, but I don't have to learn it until I get there."

"Will that be enough time?"

"Sure. It's only a one-act, and I'll have plenty of time once I'm there. I wouldn't want to tackle it while I'm trying to get Mr. Snow under my belt."

"I don't think I could do it."

"It could be worse—sometimes actors do musical summer stock where they have a week to learn a new part while they're performing the current one for that same week."

"Sounds like torture. At least with a writing deadline, you don't have to worry about memorizing."

"Oh…." This was more of a strangled whisper than a spoken word.

"What?" Mitch finally managed. "Tell me."

Grady looked stricken.

"I—I don't want to go," Grady finished.

Mitch looked up as he felt a great sinking feeling in his stomach. He didn't want Grady to go either. Figuring that is what Grady meant, Mitch gathered his spiraling wits and said quickly, "Grady, I'll miss you too. But I'll still be here, and so will your room, and when the show is over, you'll come back, and we'll just go on from there, like you've never been away. And I'll borrow Emma's car and drive up from time to time. And, of course, I'll see you in the show."

Then he ran out of words.

Grady just looked at him, wide-eyed.

"Grady," Mitch went on, "this is a great break. Something you've been working toward for a long time. You have to go."

"I know," Grady replied. "But I feel like I'm jumping off a cliff."

"I'll be here," Mitch said softly. "I'll always be here for you. You know, like you said one time you'd always be there for me. We've not become just transient friends. We're friends forever. I feel that. Don't you?"

Grady just looked at him for a long moment. "Yes," he said finally. "I feel that."

He looked more relaxed now, although Mitch's mind was in turmoil, which he struggled to conceal. Why was he so upset? He figured he'd gotten used to Grady's presence, and he admitted how much he liked it. No, perhaps it was more than like. But, as always, he didn't want to go there. Had he expected the two of them would just go on and on in a comfortable sort of limbo forever? He'd started out not wanting to give Grady the wrong impression. He didn't want to seem to be taking advantage, and he hadn't. But Grady was so loveable. Had he somehow snuck around Mitch's defenses? Mitch was not about to subject himself to soul-shattering loss again. Never. But what would life be like without Grady? Grady, with his jaunty personality and kindly traits. Had he let himself get too used to the comfort Grady provided just by being the kind of guy he was? *That's enough.* He had to put all this away for the moment and concentrate on making this separation easy for Grady.

"Grady, we have a lot of time to get ourselves used to this. Good God, we're both going through separation anxiety!"

Mitch watched Grady smile at that.

"And we'll talk on the phone as often as you like. I want you to enjoy acting in this play. This has been your aim for years. Have fun with it. When you come back, think of all the debriefing we'll have to go through. You can tell me all about what happened. How the audiences responded and all that kind of thing."

"Thank you, Mitch," Grady said seriously. "I know what you're doing, and I'll try to do as you say and enjoy this experience. I'm acting like a little kid. But I'll miss all—all our good times."

"So will I. But, as I just told you, we'll have plenty more good times once you get home."

"Home?" Grady whispered softly, almost out of hearing range.

MITCH WAS returning from taking the garbage to the compactor chute when he noticed a tall, well-dressed lady standing uncertainly at his apartment door. She raised her hand to the doorbell, but then she hesitated and pulled it back. Not wanting to startle her, Mitch stopped for a moment. Oh no, he thought, she looked like a person from some religious organization either asking for a contribution, or a proselytizer wanting to show him the true way to heaven. A perky little straw hat, with cherries at one side and a veil folded above, topped perfectly waved silver hair. A beautifully fitted dark blue suit with a ruffled light blue blouse, light blue gloves, black patent leather shoes, and a matching purse completed her outfit. She reminded him of someone, but he couldn't determine who it was. Except for her hesitation, she seemed a very put-together lady. She reached out to push the bell but then pulled her hand away again. She turned, starting back toward the stairs.

"He's not home just now," Mitch told her.

"Oh."

"Because he's right here! I'm Mitch Donnelly. Were you looking for me?"

"Oh," she said again, her mouth a perfect little circle. She wore very pale pink lipstick. "My, you're very tall, aren't you?"

"It's been said," Mitch replied, chuckling.

71

"That was a rather absurd observation," she replied, echoing his chuckle.

"Is there something I can help you with?"

"I'm Sarah."

"Sarah?" Mitch asked. "Oh." It came to him suddenly. "Sarah. Em's Sarah?"

She blushed a charming rose color. "I suppose you might say so."

"Well, come on in," Mitch told her as he opened the door for her.

She stepped in slowly and took a few minutes appraising her surroundings. Mitch shut the apartment door softly and indicated she should sit on the sofa. She crossed toward it, clutching her purse as if it were the guardrail on a very tall building. She lowered herself to the very edge of the sofa while twisting the handle of her purse, the shiny black patent leather giving off brief flashes of light. Mitch realized she was painfully uncomfortable.

"I know just what we need," Mitch declared. "Tea. That's what we need, a nice cup of tea." Without waiting for her answer, he strode into the kitchen and dug around until he found the chamomile. "Chamomile all right? Or would you like something else? I have all kinds of tea."

"Anything" came the quiet answer.

When he finally entered the living room with a teapot, two very different cups and saucers, milk and sugar, and a small plate of oatmeal cookies, all on a tray, he found her a bit more relaxed.

"Here we go," he said.

"Oh, you use different cups. So do I. It's so much more interesting."

"I inherited them from my favorite aunt. She always served tea in different cups. She collected them and wanted everyone to see as many as possible."

She blushed. "So do I."

"Can I ask you to pour?" He remembered his tea protocol from many a session with his favorite aunt. That triggered his memory. That was who she reminded him of: his Aunt Sue. She too had been a tall woman. And very particular about how she appeared in public. She'd never leave the house—and she lived in the country—without hat, purse, and gloves. She'd said she'd rather go without her underwear than without her "ensemble," as she called it. And when he thought of his Aunt Sue, he always remembered her famous homemade applesauce. It had become a sort of running joke between them. He'd told her so many times how much he loved it, how much better it was than the store-bought kind, that when he went to see her, she always had a fresh batch waiting for him. And he was being totally honest when he told her it was the best he'd ever tasted. Before passing away, she'd often sent him some here in New York. It was a great treat and reminded him of how she'd always made him feel special.

Mitch watched Sarah remove her gloves, one finger at a time, and then begin pouring the tea. When she handed Mitch his cup, it rattled a bit.

Mitch leaned forward. "Please, Sarah, don't be uncomfortable. The bits of information I've pried out of Em make me feel like I kind of know you already. Anyone who can put up with her... how shall I put it... robust personality must be a saint."

Now she did laugh, a rather hearty laugh for someone so seemingly reserved. "Emma talks about you all the time. She thinks of you as her surrogate son, you know. So I truly do know you very well."

"She's been so kind to me. We're both friends and confidants. As you suspect, we've formed a bond. And that's why I feel perfectly happy to extend that same family feeling to you. I hope you soon become that very thing. You're the best thing that's happened to Em in years!"

Mitch watched in wonder as Sarah's light blue eyes filled up. And they did not look like happy tears.

"What's wrong?" he asked, concerned.

"Well, that's pretty much why I've come to see you." She reached for her purse, opened it, and pulled out a small, gaily embroidered handkerchief. She wiped her eyes delicately.

"Yes?"

"I've grown... very fond of Emma, and I admire her, as you call it, robust personality. I'm so much the opposite. Timid. Retiring. She's like a good, gusty wind that's blown away my lingering cobwebs of uncertainty."

"A good gusty wind," Mitch repeated. "That describes her perfectly." They exchanged a long, searching look.

He watched as Sarah settled back on the sofa, now seemingly pretty much at ease. They sipped at their tea for several moments. Mitch thought it best to let Sarah take the lead. He waited for her to resume the conversation.

"That's my problem," she finally continued. "Emily expects me to be as… I suppose the correct word is… 'out' as she is. But you know my background. I was married for many years. I have a grown son. I'm the typical aging widow, filling her time with charitable work and bridge. But underneath I've always known I was simply playing a part. That I was behaving as my family, my neighbors, and society in general dictated."

"I understand."

"Let me tell you about the incident that fashioned my life from the moment it happened until now. When I was a senior in high school, my best friend was the most popular girl in school. Beautiful, she was a cheerleader, she was popular, she captained the girls' softball team. I was athletic, thank heavens, so I was on the team too. She was outgoing, brash in a nice way, much like Emma, and spoke her mind. I was the shy follower. But because of our friendship, I was included in all the parties, picnics, and beach forays. We even double-dated a lot. She always had a boyfriend, and the boyfriend always had a friend for me. We had fun. No serious entanglements."

"It sounds like she was very special to you."

"Oh, she was. She was pretty much my whole world. Anyway, we'd just come home to her house after a day at the beach with the crowd. I'd had such a good time, and I knew it was all because of her. I was so filled with gratitude… and probably feelings I didn't even understand then, and I wanted her to know how I felt. I put my arms around her and gave her a big hug. I told her I loved her dearly and was about to kiss her on the cheek when she turned toward me, and I kissed her full on the mouth."

"Oh, dear."

"Oh, dear is right. She pushed me away—very roughly and started screaming, 'Get away from me. Get out of my house. How could you? That's disgusting.' I tried to explain, but she was almost hysterical and wouldn't let me. In the end she practically pushed me down the stairs and out of her house. The last thing she said before she slammed the door was, 'I never want to see you again.'

"I was devastated. I don't know how I got home, I was crying so hard. My family wasn't home, so I went right up to my room and went to bed, where I pretty much stayed for about two weeks. My poor mother was frantic. She couldn't figure out what was wrong, and I wasn't about to tell her. Thank heavens it was only about a week until I was to graduate. Naturally, I couldn't face anyone at school, so my mother picked up my diploma. She also made me see our doctor, who, of course, couldn't find anything physically wrong with me. In desperation, I suppose, she took me to stay for a time with my aunt, her sister, and my cousin at a cabin near the sea that they'd rented for the summer. I did a lot of walking on the beach, and I think, in the end, it was that and my cousin's company that brought me back. Finally, I recovered and… life went on.

"But I was changed. I was fearful. I decided I would live a safe, conventional life. I would never, never feel like an outcast again. And so I did. And until about a year ago, I was relatively happy. But with my husband gone, the empty house and the meaningless activity, I began to feel restless and depressed. And my son had become so engrossed in his work—he always was an overachiever—that a certain distance grew between us. That's when I decided to go on the cruise, oh, just as an observer, you see. I would be just like a camcorder, recording, but not getting involved. And that worked at first. But then Emma happened."

"Like a natural phenomenon… a hurricane, perhaps?"

"She kept sitting next to my deck chair and talking to me. I couldn't be impolite and so, of course, I answered. Gradually, our rather stilted talk eased into a real conversation. I began to look forward to her coming to sit with me. It wasn't too long before we sat at the same table at dinner, and from then on were more or less inseparable.

"And the rest you know."

"It sounds like the proverbial match made in heaven."

"Yes, but you see Emma gets provoked when I'm not as bold as she is. When she wants to take my hand when we're walking down the street or in a restaurant, I can't help pulling away. And when she starts talking loud about homophobia, I ask her to quiet down. She claims I'm inhibiting her. And she's right, I am. But I can't seem to help it. I can't change the way I've behaved all these years. It's too entrenched. Emma says I'm playing old tapes in my head, and that I shouldn't give in to them. And she's probably right. But I can't be someone I'm not. At least not so fast."

"Of course you can't," Mitch reassured her. "Nobody can. Do you suppose that in time you'll feel differently?"

"I honestly don't know. I'm trying. I truly am. But when she takes my hand out on the street, my only thought is that I want to find a tree to hide behind." She laughed at herself, but it was a bitter laugh totally devoid of mirth. Then her eyes filled up and she covered her face.

Just then there was a strange scratching noise at the window, and Sarah jumped. Mitch looked over her head to see a squirrel looking in at them. That was what had caused the noise that startled Sarah, so Mitch said, "Turn around very slowly and look at the window. We have a visitor." Sarah carefully put her teacup on the side table and turned carefully. The two of them looked at the squirrel, and the squirrel looked back. Then with a swish of its fluffy gray tail, it jumped back to the tree.

"He's come for his afternoon snack," Mitch told her. "I gave him a peanut once, and he seems to think this is an ongoing affair. He shows up almost every day for his treat. And I haven't the heart to disappoint him."

Mitch stood up and crossed to the window. From a package on the sill, he took a peanut. After pulling up the window, with only a slight screech, he laid the peanut in the middle of the sill and stepped back. The fresh breeze tickled his face in a refreshing burst. After a long look at Mitch, the little squirrel darted forward, snatched the peanut, and jumped back into the tree. Mitch closed the window with a chuckle and returned to the sofa.

"Cute. I was so surprised to learn that squirrels are part of the rodent family," Sarah told him.

"Me too," Mitch replied. "And I had a friend once who had a ferret for a pet, and I always thought they were a 'stretch rat,' as they say, but they're feline, related to cats."

Sarah smiled momentarily, but then the sad cast returned to her face.

Mitch got up and sat beside her on the sofa. He took her hand. "Sarah, all you can do is try. I think Em has to understand and at least meet you halfway. Have you told her about your horrible experience in high school?"

"Oh yes. But she can't understand how something that happened so long ago can still affect me. Nothing has ever seemed to bother her, and she really doesn't care what people think of her."

"Oh, don't I know. But if a person hasn't experienced such a horrible thing, they can't really understand the entrenched ways of a person who has."

She gripped his hand tightly. "I'm afraid she's going to leave me."

"Oh no, Em will never let that happen. I hear how she talks about you, and I hear the tone of her voice. I know her to be fiercely devoted to someone she cares about. She may crab at you from time to time, but she'd never desert you. Never."

"Well," Sarah said, "you've made me feel better. Thank you for listening to my history. You're a kind man. Just what Emma has told me."

"Anytime you want to talk, please come back, and we'll have another tea party. I think, totally aside from Em, we understand each other."

"Yes," she said, and she smiled, a true smile, for the first time.

She's a real charmer, he thought, as he couldn't help smiling back.

LATER, WHEN Mitch was in the kitchen, busy washing the window over the kitchen sink and looking out at the plants in the garden below, he heard the front door open and close. Grady was home. Mitch dropped the Windex and the cloth on the drainboard and joined him in the living room to fill him in on Sarah's visit.

"Oh, the poor thing," Grady said. They sat on either end of the sofa. "It's awful to be uncertain about how much you mean to somebody you care about."

There was a rather strange look on Grady's face that Mitch couldn't quite interpret. In a split second it was gone, and Mitch wondered if he'd imagined it.

"And given her background and that tragic rejection so early in life, she's especially vulnerable," Mitch added. "You know, I hate to meddle, but I think I need to have a serious talk with Em. Sometimes she's so focused on what she thinks that she misses all the nuances around her. I don't think she'd want Sarah to be so unhappy."

"Great, if you think you wouldn't get your head chopped off and fed bit by bit to Tweet."

Mitch laughed. "Em is like a walnut—tough, but if you crack the shell, you'll find a marshmallow inside. It took me a while to realize that all her brashness covers a very soft heart. She would never cause Sarah any pain if she knew she was doing it."

"You're probably right. But better you than me."

Their talk was interrupted by the ringing of the doorbell.

"Maybe that's her," Grady said.

"No, that's not her ring."

Mitch unfolded his lanky frame and headed toward the door, stopping to flip a corner of the rug back down with one foot as he passed. He opened the door, and his spirits plummeted like a water bucket dropped into a well. There, with a vapid grin on his face, stood his former friend, Brandon. Dressed in an ill-fitting blue suit with a yellow polka-dotted bow tie and carrying a battered suitcase, he looked little like the fashion-conscious teenager Mitch had once known. Apparently ugly clothes went right along with righting one's orientation. Probably something about modesty, if past conversations were any indication.

Mitch had to suppress the urge to slam the door in his face and go back to the sofa in peace. But Brandon was, after all, an old friend, albeit an unwelcome one.

"Hello, Mitch," Brandon said with what sounded to Mitch like a fake bonhomie, "aren't you going to ask me in?"

"Uh… sure. Come on in, Brandon. I figured you'd call first before showing up."

"I wanted to surprise you."

Blindside him, was more like it. Mitch stepped aside, and Brandon walked into the apartment. It had been a while since his last visit, and Mitch had been in his old apartment then. He watched Brandon take in his surroundings and frown critically.

"Well, how bohemian" was his opinion.

"Really. You were expecting *Architectural Digest*?"

"It's not the kind of furnishings we grew up with." Brandon dropped his suitcase with a thud. The sudden noise caused Grady to stand up. Brandon looked at him for a long moment before turning to Mitch.

"And who is this?" he asked.

"This is my good friend, Grady Gilmore. Grady, this is Brandon Willis. We were neighbors for many years."

Grady stepped forward, his hand outstretched, which Brandon shook quickly, looking quite uncomfortable. To Mitch, he seemed like he wanted to wipe his hand on his trousers. Mitch felt tired suddenly. He'd been through this sort of thing with Brandon on many occasions, and he didn't want to go there again, particularly with Grady in attendance.

Grady sat back down, and Mitch indicated that Brandon should sit on the other end of the sofa. Brandon, instead, chose one of the chairs, so Mitch joined Grady on the sofa. Silence reigned for a time. Grady looked at Mitch again with a mixture of amusement and confusion.

"And what kind of work do you do… Grady, was it?"

"He's an actor," Mitch supplied.

"And I also work at a law firm doing PowerPoint presentations."

"How… interesting. And do you live here in the Village also?"

"Grady's staying with me for the time being," Mitch said.

"Oh. Is he that kind of 'friend'?"

"Don't start, Brandon," Mitch warned.

"You think you can fool me, don't you," he said, sitting on the edge of the chair. "But I see the looks you give each other. I know that kind of look. You fancy yourselves in love with each other. It's painfully obvious."

Mitch was startled into silence at first and looked quickly at Grady, who just as quickly looked away. Was he upset that anyone might misinterpret his relationship with Mitch? Or could it be—

"Look, Brandon," Mitch said through almost gritted teeth, "I told you, don't start. Grady is my friend. And even if he were more than that, it's no business of yours!"

"But it is. Mitch, I've tried so hard to make you see the errors of your lifestyle, but you won't listen to the truth. And now you calmly introduce me to your boyfriend and pretend he's just a friend. Just a friend, indeed. You think I can't tell? I can see the truth—"

"The truth? Some kind of fake truth you've convinced yourself to believe. Brandon, you've been brainwashed. A person doesn't go from liking guys at sixteen to liking girls at seventeen. It just doesn't happen. And at some level you know it."

"I know that I've changed. And you can too. Lying with a man is an abomination. It says so in the Bible!"

"Yes, in the same passage that says it's a sin to wear clothes made of two different types of cloth. I believe your suit is a blend. Does that mean you're going to hell?"

"You're just trying to change the subject."

"No, I'm not letting you be selective with your Bible quotes. The Leviticus verse you quote from is full of such nonsense. You people just pick the part that suits your prejudices. How about touching the skin of a dead pig makes you unclean? No gloves, shoes, jackets, and heaven help you if you throw a football. Think of all those abominations that everyone watches every weekend, rooting for the home team. That's the same Leviticus you quote so freely."

Grady interrupted. "Look, why don't we talk about something else? Okay?"

"You keep out of this," Brandon almost snarled. "You may be Mitch's 'special friend,' but I've known him for years. I'm trying to save my friend. You're probably the one keeping him away from redemption. You've probably convinced him he loves you!"

Was it love he felt for Grady? Maybe it was…. *Oh no, just stop thinking, right this minute!* Mitch was so stunned the argument became a buzz in his ears. The words kept echoing in his ears. Had he fallen in love with Grady without even realizing it? Had he, in fact, fallen in love with Grady while actively fighting not to? The feeling of impending loss started to choke him, but his feelings for Grady couldn't be denied. And wasn't fear of loss a problem for everybody? The title of the song "Everybody Hurts" ran through his mind. But it was followed by the part about holding on. Maybe that's what he had to do. He would hold on. He'd hold on to Grady and just let events take him wherever they chose. The fear of loss subsided until Mitch actually felt elated. Did he love again? Was he in love with Grady? What a mess.

But… what if Grady didn't feel the same? After all, Grady had had a terrible shock. Would it even be possible for him to love again so soon? They got along so well. They fit somehow. But that was only liking someone, even someone special. Should he even dare to hope? His reverie was interrupted by the jangling notes of the doorbell. As he snapped out of his trance and hurried to the door, he heard Grady say, "Mitch is the most empathic, understanding man I've ever met. He's a great guy. I don't care if he's in love with a panda bear!"

He had to smile as he swung the door open, and Emma rushed in, her wig a dark brown upsweep from the forties.

"What's all the yelling about?" she demanded.

Brandon, seeing Emma, someone older, obviously convinced he now had an ally, started toward her, followed by Grady.

"I've been trying to show these two the error of their ways. I don't want my poor friend Mitch being influenced by this disgusting fag!"

Mitch watched Emma stand stiffly for a moment, much like a steel rod. Then she walked up to Brandon, stood up on her toes, and slapped him soundly across the face.

"You little shit!" she hollered. "How dare you use such language in my presence? I want you out of here. Right now. This may be Mitch's apartment, but this is my building, and I won't have a bigoted homophobe on my premises. Get out now, or I'll whack you again!" She raised her hand to let him know she meant every word.

Brandon stumbled back, his hand covering the red mark on his cheek, grabbed his suitcase, and after circling around the chairs, keeping Emma as far away as possible, he scuttled to the door and opened it.

"You're all going to burn in hell! Abominations, all of you!" he shouted and quickly slammed the door before anyone could get to him, although Emma tried. Mitch took hold of her arm.

"Em, he's not worth it."

The three of them stood in absolute silence for a long time. Finally Mitch went to the window and pulled the bottom sash up with a screech.

"I've got to air the place out after that," he remarked, turning back to the other two. "What a stink he left."

That seemed to break the tension, and they all relaxed. Grady and Emma returned to the sofa while Mitch started for the kitchen.

"I think we all need a big hunk of chocolate to lift our spirits."

"Chocolate is good," Grady agreed.

"What a piece of work that one is," Emma offered.

"Actually, I feel sorry for him," Mitch said as he returned with a square of chocolate for each of them along with plenty of napkins (white canvas furniture being white canvas furniture). He took a big bite of chocolate, relishing the viscous melting, and then continued, "He wasn't always like that. His parents sent him to some reparative-therapy camp, and they got him into some sort of denial. I keep hoping he'll come to his senses. I've tried to convince him he can't really change, but he literally puts his hands over his ears so he can't hear me."

"Well," Grady conceded, "I guess I can forgive him."

"Well, I can't," Emma offered. "We've come too far for people like that to keep attacking us all the time. I remember a time when you could get arrested for being in a gay bar—not that I was much for bars, but it's the principle of the thing."

"That seems barbaric by today's standards."

"It was barbaric by any standards," Emma stated emphatically.

And that was the last word on the subject.

THE NEXT day was peaceful. At least, it was peaceful on the outside. Inside Mitch's head, turmoil raged. Had he somehow fallen for Grady? He suspected that he had. Should he say anything to Grady? It was going to be very difficult keeping his emotions under check now that he realized there was some deep emotion under the surface. He was so very inclined to take Grady in his arms and blurt out his newly discovered feelings. But if Grady didn't have similar feelings, it would become horribly awkward. And at this point Mitch didn't want anything to upset the comfortable routine they'd established. And, anyway, was he completely sure? He'd only mentioned love to one person in his whole life, Jared, and he'd always felt a person should be absolutely and positively sure of his feelings before mentioning that loaded word.

He'd tried getting lost in his writing but couldn't seem to put two sentences together. Oh, he'd tried before Grady left for rehearsals, and while he ran his fingers over the keyboard very convincingly, when he reviewed what he'd written after Grady left, it made no sense. It was strictly stream of consciousness. He'd paced the apartment enough to cover the distance of a marathon. Finally, late in the afternoon, exhausted, he'd thrown himself on the sofa and fallen asleep.

"Ah," he heard later through a distant fog, "what have we here? A sleeping beauty. Would a kiss wake him up, do you think? Perhaps I should see."

He came to suddenly to see Grady's face close enough to his own that his warm breath wafted across his cheek. Startled, he scuttled backward and rose up on his elbows.

"Grady?" he asked fuzzily. "I was just resting for a bit." He saw Grady frown. It looked like he was disappointed. Grady stood up, took off his jacket, and crossed the room to open the window. The rush of fresh air did much to clear Mitch's mind. He realized it was hot in the apartment. He'd forgotten to turn the air conditioner back on before he passed out. No wonder he felt fuzzy in the head. The room seemed heavy, the air almost like a solid thing.

"It's not like you to sleep in the middle of the day," Grady told him. "I was afraid that our recent lovely scene with your old friend might be bothering you more than we thought."

"No, although he makes me crazy, I usually end up feeling sorry for him. He was so different when we were kids. Actually, what happened… I reached a sticking point in my writing, and I escaped into sleep." Mitch felt bad making up something to excuse any strange behavior, but better that than having Grady notice something was not quite right with him emotionally. He sat up on the sofa and ran his hands through his hair.

"The writer's curse?" Grady said. Mitch heard his footsteps crossing from the window to the back of the sofa. Then he felt Grady's warm hands on his shoulders.

"Mitch, you are so tense. Your shoulders feel like iron girders." Grady began using his strong thumbs to massage the stiffness away.

"Ah," Mitch murmured, "that feels so good."

Too good. Way too good.

His blood began to pound in his head, and his heart started behaving like a jazz drummer. He could swear Grady must feel it. He endured it as long as he was able and then suddenly stood up.

"I—I need a couple of aspirins and some water." He hurried into the kitchen, got the aspirin out of one of the cabinets, and got some ice water out of the refrigerator. The whoosh of cold air was a relief to his overheated face, both from the heat in the apartment and the touch of Grady's hands.

Grady followed him into the kitchen, pulled out one of the chairs from the table, and sat down. He picked up a bunch of grapes from the bowl of fruit sitting on the table and popped one into his mouth.

"How was rehearsal?" Mitch asked quickly.

"Okay. It's a really good cast, and the director blocked the first act. Along with having friends in the cast, the Desdemona is terrific. She's playing it like I always thought it should be played."

"How's that?"

"Very strong. Desdemona seems to always be played as a sort of shrinking violet. But the woman has defied her father and the whole court to stand by her choice of a Moor for her husband. Pretty gutsy, I've always thought."

"You're right. That's how I saw her when I reread the play."

"You reread the play?"

"Well, of course. If you're going to be in it, I want to know everything about it. I even read some critical writings."

"Well… well, that's great. I don't want you to take up time from your writing, though."

"I think reading Shakespeare can only help my writing."

"There is that. But I'm still impressed."

"Good," Mitch teased. "Impressed is good. Tell me more about the rehearsal."

"Well, Patty's Emilia is perfection. I think that's one of the great female parts in Shakespeare, if it's played right. Her reaction to Desdemona dying can be a real tearjerker. Here's this army wife, this tough broad, falling to pieces over her husband's betrayal. When she says, 'My husband, my husband'… well, when Patty got to that point, even in the read-through, I got chills up my spine. I think it's going to be a smashing production."

"I'm so happy for you, Grady. I think you really deserve something special."

"Thanks, Mitch. There's still a little problem, but I think I took care of it."

"What's that?"

"Well, Randall started coming on to me again."

"Am I going to have to kill someone?"

"Thanks, but no. I told him again that I'm committed."

"Oh?"

There followed an awkward silence.

The doorbell rang and two knocks followed.

"That's Em's ring," Mitch said, quickly rising. "I'll get it."

He hurried to the door and opened it as Emma rushed in.

"Well, how're my fellow abominations today?"

"Abominable, of course."

"Just like the snowman!"

"Right."

"Is Grady home?"

"Yes, we were in the kitchen. He was telling me about his rehearsal for *Othello*."

"Ah," said Em, "That I did love the Moor to live with him, my downright violence and storm of fortunes may trumpet to the world. My heart's subdued even to the very quality of my lord. I saw Othello's visage in his mind, and to his honors and his valiant parts did I my soul and fortunes consecrate."

"Wow!" Grady said.

"I wasn't an English teacher for nothing."

"But direct quotes," Mitch said as he watched Emma straighten the pillows on the sofa as they passed en route to the kitchen.

"Pour me a glass of that red stuff you always have on hand. I'm real parched. Grady, dear, how are you?"

"Abominable!"

They all gave a hearty laugh as Emma jumped up and sat on the drainboard.

"I wish you'd sit at the table like a lady," Mitch told her.

"First off, I've never claimed to be a lady. And second, this is my one chance to be taller than everyone."

"Touché," Grady said.

"Right," Mitch replied. "If we'd ever dueled with real swords, I'd be long dead."

"As I keep mentioning, I was an English teacher. With teenagers, you get very good at comebacks. Now, Grady, tell me about your rehearsal."

"Well," Mitch cut in grimly, "he's already got an admirer."

"Oh," she replied, "and what did our Mitch say about that?"

"Well, he did mention murder."

"See? I told you so!"

"What?" Grady asked.

Mitch realized that Emma had figured out immediately that there was attraction between him and Grady, and now he knew she was right, but Grady couldn't read her as well as he could.

Mitch interjected quickly, "How about Em quoting one of Desdemona's lines when she came in, from memory yet. Pretty impressive...."

Emma gave him a rather smug (he thought) smile, as if saying she'd let him off the hook for now.

"Well, if we need an understudy to take over," Grady said, "we'll know where we can find one."

"Right," Emma said, "I could maybe pull off the duke, but not Desdemona. Maybe a few years ago...."

"I think Desdemona was just as feisty as you are. Mitch and I were just talking about it."

"I agree," Em said. "I guess it's true that great minds think alike."

"Em," Mitch said reluctantly, "we need to have a little talk."

"Okay. What about?"

"I'm going to change into something more comfortable," Grady said, wiggling his eyebrows suggestively.

"That's my boy. So tactful," Emma said as Grady left. "Well?" she added after a moment.

"It's Sarah. She came to see me."

"Sarah came to see you," she repeated in a monotone.

"Now stay calm. If you jump on me from up there, we could both end up with broken bones."

"But... why?"

"She's a dear person, by the way, but she's terrified she's going to lose you."

"Lose me? No way can she lose me."

Emma did slip off the drainboard and came to sit opposite him at the table. She sipped the last dregs from her glass and set it on the table.

"She's afraid she's too timid for you."

"I think she's cute. She gets embarrassed so easily."

"I know, but when you grab her hand in public and she pulls away, she thinks you don't understand that her background makes her skittish."

"Well, I know that. The woman wears gloves and carries a purse. She plays classical piano."

"What's that got to do with it?"

"She's old-fashioned. I'm just trying to bring her into this century."

"She sees herself as being too frightened of what others will think. She wishes she were more like you."

"If she were more like me, I probably wouldn't like her."

Mitch had to laugh at that. That caused Emma to smile ruefully.

"We had a cup of tea… and she cried."

"Oh, Mitch," Emma said, truly upset. "What have I done? I wouldn't cause her even a moment's unhappiness. I just thought I could help her feel better about her… about us."

"I know that. I know you. By the end of our talk she seemed reassured. I don't mean to interfere, but I thought you'd want to hear about it."

"Of course. We're family, Mitch. You know what's good for me, just like I know"—and here she tossed her head toward Grady's room—"what's good for you."

Mitch chose not to comment. "My squirrel visited, and I think that helped us both feel more comfortable with each other. She was smiling when I gave him a peanut, and things lightened up after that."

"Squirrels are good for that. No, I'm so glad you told me. I'll have to stop the"—here she put finger quotes around her words—"'public displays of affection' gradually. Otherwise she'll figure out we've talked. She's very smart."

"And very sweet. She's a lot like Caro, you realize."

"You're saying I have a type? Well, I do. So what? Sweetness helps leaven my acidic wit."

"Hear, hear!"

Emma slapped him lightly on the wrist.

"You don't have to agree with me."

"I do if I don't want a tongue-lashing."

Grady entered the room wearing Levi's and a snug blue T-shirt. Mitch noticed the blue matched his eyes. Lord, he was getting positively maudlin.

"Gee," Grady said, "I didn't even hear any crockery smashing."

"We only traded words," Emma told him. "Not solid objects."

"Not yet," Mitch said.

"I've got to go," Emma told them, rising from the table. "Sarah and I are going out to dinner. I'll see myself out."

And the whirlwind was gone.

"She doesn't realize it, but she always shows herself out," Mitch said. "No one can keep up with her."

"I take it your little talk went well?"

"Perfectly. Poor Em had no idea. She thought she was doing the right thing."

"Yes," Grady replied, "we all make that mistake sometimes."

Chapter Six

WITHOUT COMING to any conclusion, and opting for safety, Mitch let the days fall into the same pattern they had before Brandon's ill-timed visit and any revelations that had ensued. Grady would work, come home, go over his lines with Mitch, and then head out to rehearsal. Mitch felt he could easily do Othello's part; he had inadvertently learned those lines as well. He worked on his novel constantly, and though thoughts of his dilemma with Grady intruded often, he forced the thoughts from his mind. He didn't want to try to solve anything with Grady going away so soon. His work went fairly well, considering the fractured state of his mind.

And then opening night was upon them. Mitch, along with Em and Sarah, had front-row seats.

"I'm so nervous," Grady said as he got ready.

"Why?" Mitch asked. "You surely have your lines. I should know."

"Doesn't make any difference. I always get nervous. I was marked forever by my first play. It was only a small part when I was a freshman in college. I was playing the part of the sheriff in *Bus Stop*. All I really had was a little monologue near the end. We'd actually done several performances, and everything went perfectly well. Then on closing night, I put my foot up on a chair, as I'd been blocked to do, leaned my elbow on my knee, and went absolutely blank."

"Oh, my God. In front of an audience."

"Right. I was more surprised than upset... at first. I remember thinking that I knew the lines, but no matter how hard I tried, I simply couldn't remember them. The silence was thunderous. I heard whispers from the wings as people tried to feed me the lines, but I couldn't hear them, although I'm sure the audience did."

"What did you do?"

"I felt like running off the stage and never going back to school. But suddenly the lines popped into my head, I delivered them, and the play zoomed on to the end. I wouldn't even take my curtain call I was so embarrassed. And that, my friend, left me marked for life. I'm always afraid it'll happen again."

"Has it?"

"No. But that doesn't stop the nerves."

"Why do you keep on doing it?" Mitch asked.

"I suppose for the same reason you kept on writing after getting rejections. I can't *not* do it! And once I'm onstage, all the nerves disappear."

"Good comparison. I understand completely," Mitch replied. "Well, I know you told me never to wish you good luck as, for some reason, that's tempting bad luck so I'll just say, 'Knock 'em dead!'"

"Thanks." Grady held out his arms. "Give me a hug for good luck."

Mitch stepped forward, took Grady in his arms, and squeezed him. He felt so good.

When his heart started beating double time, Mitch pulled back. "Go on. You don't want to be late. We'll be along in a little while. Em's even dressing up for the great event."

"Wow. I'm honored."

And then he was gone.

Mitch felt empty and alone.

Dammit, anyway.

MITCH WAS just slipping on the jacket of what he called his "interview with an agent suit," a dark blue vintage Bill Blass, when his doorbell gave the Emma signal: a ring followed by two sharp knocks. He opened the door to find a resplendent Em in a black satin pantsuit, low-heeled patent leather pumps, a variegated black-shading-to-white scarf, and emerald earrings that had been Caro's. Sarah, with a huge smile on her face, matched Emma's splendor in every way. In a beautiful dark blue shantung cocktail dress, black velvet high-heeled shoes and a gold jewelry set of earrings, necklace and bracelet, she clutched a black velvet purse in gloved hands.

"Wow!" Mitch exclaimed as he stepped out to meet them. "I'm blinded by the elegance of it all!"

"You don't look too shabby yourself," Em replied as she took one of his arms and Sarah took the other.

"You look very, very nice," Sarah said softly.

Then they were rushing out.

On the porch Mitch felt as if the balmy evening had been made just for them. A light breeze brushed his cheek, and there was a distinct floral smell in the air instead of the usual mix of garbage and car exhaust. So far this was turning out to be a perfect evening.

As they started down the stairs, both Em and Sarah suddenly stopped, as if they'd run into a glass wall, and both stared at the shiny white stretch limousine pulling up to the curb. The driver hopped out, circled the car, and opened the back door for them.

"Oh my," said Sarah, "I've never been in one! How luxurious."

"Oh, Mitch," Em said, rather breathlessly for her. "First class."

"Nothing is too good for lovely ladies like you two. We should ride in a grubby cab?" He clutched their arms tighter to his sides as they hurried down the stairs and into the car. The soft white leather seats cradled them gently. The subtle track lighting below the windows gave off an almost candle-like luminescence. This was true luxury, and Mitch figured it was worth every penny as he watched the two women's reactions. He couldn't keep himself from smiling.

As the windows were tinted, it turned outside objects an unpleasant olive green, so Mitch stopped looking out. In no time at all they were pulling up in front of what looked like a converted storefront. There was a dark blue awning, obviously quite new, with glass showcases on either side of the door, holding posters for the show. The doorway appeared to have been enlarged and sported a large wooden door, stained dark walnut.

There was a small crowd outside on the sidewalk, all of which stared at the elegant trio emerging from the limo. Em was in her element, almost as if she expected autograph hunters; Sarah was quietly embarrassed. Mitch leaned more toward Sarah's reaction than toward Em's.

They entered the lobby, and Mitch's attention was immediately drawn to the cast photos on the wall. There was Grady smiling at him. He looked so handsome.

At the small box office window, Mitch mentioned his name, and the young girl passed over an envelope containing their complimentary tickets. At the door to the theater, Mitch handed the tickets to the usher, another young girl, who escorted them to the very first row and indicated the three middle seats. Mitch maneuvered Em to the center so she could sit next to Sarah. He felt an unruly bunch of woodpeckers fighting over space just under his breastbone. If this was a tenth what Grady felt, Mitch appreciated all over again how dedicated an actor he must be to continue seeking this torture. Em and Sarah were reading Em's program together.

"Mitch," Em stated, "Grady's done a lot of acting. His bio is quite impressive."

Mitch swelled with pride. "He's really very, very good, and I'm not just saying that because he's my friend. When I hear him run his lines, he actually scares me."

"Dear Grady scares you?" Sarah said.

"Dear Grady disappears, and this evil creature emerges. It's uncanny."

Mitch noticed they had built (as Grady had explained to him) a unit set of stark boxes and columns painted black with swabs of red and white. There was a foreboding feel to the whole set, along with strange streams of light, heavily into ambers and blues. The modern twist had been abandoned in favor of traditional costuming.

Suddenly the lights began to dim, and there was a rustle as the audience settled down. Then an almost eerie silence descended, the usual hush before the performance of a play. When the lights came up, most of the cast was already on stage.

Grady entered between two tall pillars with the actor playing Roderigo.

Mitch barely recognized Grady with a sword at his side, black tights, a gold-and-black tunic, and a black cape with a gold lining framing his usually familiar body. Makeup cast a whole different fierce look to his features, and his hair was styled, shiny, and very flat to his head. His gait was different, and soon Mitch noticed his gestures were also.

Even so altered, he was still so handsome. How could he ever be interested in Mitch?

Mitch was surprised to feel despair. He had no time to ponder his feelings, as his attention was drawn back to the stage as the actor playing Roderigo uttered his first lines.

"Tush! Never tell me; I take it much unkindly that thou, Iago, who hast had my purse as if the strings were thine, shouldst know of this."

Then Grady spoke for the first time.

"S'blood, but you will not hear me. If ever I did dream of such a matter, abhor me."

His voice took on a smooth, velvety quality that managed to be insidious at the same time. Mitch was entranced. This was Grady, but not Grady, such was his acting ability. Mitch was awed. Looks, talent, and kindness of heart—what a guy!

The action sped on. Othello was, indeed, excellent: tall, lithe, with a confident, almost heroic carriage. He exuded the quality of a general. Desdemona was not only beautiful but also strong as she explained her love for Othello and why she felt so. And Grady's friend Patty was magnificent as Emilia. Of course, he hated Cassio on sight. The guy was handsome, all right. Blond curls, Caesar-like, above startling blue eyes. Tall, with a swagger. And this bird had tried hitting on Grady! Mitch felt himself devoured by the most acute jealousy. This was not good!

Mitch was soon lost in the action on stage, fully accepting the treacherous duality that Grady portrayed as Iago. He forgot, almost, that it was Grady up there.

And then the action came to the end of Act 2, Scene 3, and the speech Grady had practiced in front of Mitch many times, always causing him to push back into the sofa to escape consummate evil. Grady rested on the stage, arm casually slung over one of the square blocks comprising part of the set. As he'd told Mitch he would, he gestured a bit with his free hand, looked up, riveting the audience, and began.

"And what's he then that says I play the villain?"

Mitch was fascinated watching Grady perform the speech he'd heard so often. It was even better than any he'd heard before in rehearsal—polished, so reasonable, yet so unsettling. He noticed vaguely that the audience was absolutely still, not a sound, not a cough, nothing. Then came the dramatic moment of change, when Iago's true nature exploded.

"Divinity—of Hell!" he spat, rising to one knee.

Even though Mitch knew what was coming, he was shocked. He heard Em's quick intake of breath and the little scream that Sarah let out. Once again, he felt the need to get away. Away from this hideous rage. On and on Grady ranted until his last words were hissed just like a snake. There was a blackout, and then the house lights came up for an intermission. What could possibly follow that?

The audience needed a break to regroup. The three friends sat for several moments, collecting themselves. Most of the audience seemed to be doing the same thing. Then the buzz began, and Mitch heard snatches of speech praising Grady's performance. One man, in particular, told his companions that he'd seen many productions of *Othello*, his favorite Shakespeare, and this was the best Iago he'd ever seen. Mitch filed that away to relate to Grady later as he led the ladies up the worn carpet into the crowded lobby. He spotted a refreshment counter.

"Would you like a drink or something?" he asked.

"No, thanks," Em replied with a wry look. "Actually, nature calls. And, as usual there's a huge line in front of the ladies' and none in front of the men's."

With a snort of derision, she set off through the crowd. Sarah, blushing even under the subdued lighting, followed behind her.

Mitch smiled even as he sympathized. He knew he'd feel embarrassed if he had to stand in a line of guys with everyone knowing the possible agony he was suffering. But eventually they were back.

"Well, that was a lovely experience," Em stated. "The restroom was covered in fake fur!"

Sarah giggled. "I thought it was kind of cute… just as long as it was fake."

As they started back into the theater, trying to avoid the last-minute crush, Mitch told them, "I don't think I'd like a furry restroom on a daily basis." He was glad the theater had air-conditioning, as he knew with that many people it would not be comfortable without it, and heat would detract from the action on the stage. They'd barely settled down when the house lights went on and off several times. Those lingering rushed back in, and soon the play resumed. It sped to its inevitable ending.

The three of them shed no tears, which meant that the play had, indeed, come off as a true tragedy. Mitch remembered from a college course that in Aristotle's Poetics, in a true tragedy—unlike a melodrama, such as *Romeo and Juliet*, where if only this had happened or that had occurred, the tragedy could have been avoided—the course is set, and through the main character's own weakness, he brings about his own comeuppance. An audience, according to Aristotle, should experience pity, but no tears.

GRADY, NOW out of costume and makeup, flew off the stage and into Mitch's arms.

Mitch gave him a fierce hug and whispered in his ear, "You were... the only word is, magnificent."

"Aw, Mitch," Grady whispered back, his breath brushing Mitch's ear and causing him a sudden shiver.

Then Grady turned to Em and Sarah and gave each a hug and a big kiss on the cheek. The compliments flowed, and Grady, though obviously pleased, could only look at the floor.

"I have to stay for the party. It's only a gathering onstage for nibbles and wine, and I'll get away as soon as I can. I'd rather celebrate with you guys."

"Don't feel pressured to leave," Mitch cautioned, but he fervently wished otherwise.

"No trouble. It was a great cast, but we really didn't have time to bond much offstage. I won't stay any longer than I have to. I just want to have a few words with Patty."

"Okay," Em said, "we'll take our magic carriage and go home and wait for your triumphant entrance."

"English teacher," Mitch said.

Sarah stepped forward, as if to support Em, and actually took hold of her hand.

"I know she must have been a great teacher," Sarah said.

"I was."

"And modest," Mitch added and got a slap on the hand.

"Tell your friend, Patty, we thought she was great too," Em said.

They took their leave and returned to the waiting limo to be driven back to the Village.

ONCE HOME, the limo dismissed, Em and Sarah sat on the sofa discussing the play while Mitch went to check on the champagne. He reappeared holding the bottle, which looked properly ridiculous housed in an ice-filled little orange plastic bucket. He also balanced in his other hand a small cake (chocolate, naturally) that he'd ordered from a local bakery. Mitch could bake great already prepared chocolate chip cookies, but that was the extent of his culinary skills.

"That bucket definitely does not go with a stretch limousine," Em said.

"It's all I have. I got it filled with something or other at a promotion."

"You know who I felt sorriest for in the play?" Sarah said.

"Who?" Em answered.

"Emilia. To be so completely disillusioned about your husband would be awful. To discover the person you've shared your life with is capable of such horrid behavior would be devastating."

"I wonder if Grady noticed the similarity to his own recent unpleasantness?" Em said. "Although Emilia's disillusion was far worse, any disillusion of that kind would be shattering."

"He was pretty shattered," Mitch said, and then he changed the subject. "I hope this little cake is all right. Grady is so careful with the calories."

"I like the star in the middle with Grady's name on it," Sarah said.

"After tonight's performance, it's certainly apropos," Em answered.

Then they heard Grady's keys searching for the lock. Em quickly turned off the lights with the remote she'd been clutching as Mitch lit the single candle in the middle of the star on the cake.

They were all standing in the dim candlelight when Grady stepped through the door. They clapped riotously, and Sarah declared several "Bravos." The surprise and delight on Grady's face told them he was, indeed, most pleased at this little tribute.

Mitch poured the champagne into flutes and cut the cake. The four of them began to discuss the play and their reactions.

"I thought it was a very talented cast," Em said.

"Me too. Especially you, Grady. And Emilia," Sarah added.

"I thought they were all great," Mitch said. "Except for Cassio."

"You didn't like Cassio?" Grady asked.

"No. I thought he was much too good-looking," Mitch joked. He realized, however, that beneath the joke was a bit of truth.

"He was rather plain… compared to our Grady," Em said.

"You two," Grady replied. Then he said, "This cake is really good."

And so the evening progressed, with Sarah now sitting in one of the big chairs with Em perched on the arm, proving that she did like to be taller than everyone if she got the chance. But finally the ladies took their leave, and when Mitch turned from the door, Grady had lain back on the sofa and was fast asleep.

Mitch removed Grady's shoes and carefully put his feet on the sofa. He went and got a blanket and put it gently over Grady's sleeping form. He felt an almost consuming wave of tenderness take hold of him, and he leaned over and carefully pushed a lock of Grady's lustrous brown hair off his forehead and back into place. His hand lingered on the side of Grady's face for several long moments. Oh, God, he shouldn't let this happen

If nothing else, it wouldn't be fair to Grady, who'd just gotten through the traumatic separation from Hank and wouldn't be up to any emotional involvement. For once the paralyzing fear of loss was nowhere in the picture. He didn't notice its absence—he was too worried about hurting Grady.

He walked away quietly to his lonely bed.

THE NEXT morning Mitch was up early, having slept only fitfully. He'd finished his usual breakfast and was sitting at his computer trying to finish the latest chapter in his book, but his mind was… completely blank. Blank, that is, to any words for his book. Otherwise, his mind was in turmoil. After the realization of the night before, he felt he just had to curb his growing feelings for Grady. If he said anything at this point it would look like he was taking advantage of Grady's recently wounded spirit. He would put Grady in a terrible spot; perhaps he would think Mitch's kindness expected some sort of payback. And Mitch would not have a thought like that even slip through Grady's mind. Well, it was only the rest of this week, and then the next until Grady had to leave for *Carousel*. Surely he could manage to be discreet for that long. But it certainly wouldn't be easy.

"What wouldn't?" Grady asked as he came through the door in his snow-white terry-cloth robe.

Mitch realized he'd actually spoken out loud. "Ah… finishing this chapter. It's been a difficult one. Reminds me of an old country western song, something about rocks in the road." Mitch looked up and saw Grady's beautifully sculpted chest peeking through the top of the robe. Mitch's stomach did its imitation of a roller coaster just tipping over the top of the first incline. He wondered if he might have "gulped" like cartoon figures always did when shocked.

"I wish I could give you some mental dynamite," Grady said.

"Nice thought. How are you feeling this morning, after your triumph?"

"Come on, Mitch, you're going to give me a swelled head."

"I doubt that. But, seriously, you were… what's the right word? Superb."

"Mitch, I—"

"No, Em agreed with me, and she's been to about a thousand plays. She said she was enthralled. Grady, you are so talented. Something's going to break for you. I just know it."

"Thanks, Mitch," Grady replied softly. His blue eyes held a look that gave Mitch a frisson up his spine that felt like it might just keep going right through the ceiling.

"Was the director pleased?" he said quickly, looking down at his blank screen. "I know that somewhere the author sure was."

Grady smiled. "The director seemed to be in seventh heaven. At the party he made a little speech that was really touching. Patty had tears in her eyes. Of course, Cassio had to spoil everything by muttering, 'That's sure not Shakespeare!'"

"Well, he's no Laurence Olivier!"

"Who is?"

"As I said, you might be."

"Mitch...."

"All right, I'll keep quiet, but I won't stop thinking it. So Cassio is a real stinker?"

"He kept hitting on me, until I told him I simply wasn't interested and to leave me alone. You'd think no one had ever turned him down, he seemed so surprised. He's so aware of his good looks. Patty has been in a couple of plays with him, and she told me he brags about his allure, that he always sets out to get a boyfriend in any play he's cast in, a sort of trophy, for the duration of the play, and then dumps them. With me he kept right on trying to be charming, until Patty, bless her heart, hollered at him to quit it in front of everyone. He stopped, but then he started making snide remarks to me when nobody could hear him. I finally grabbed him and told him if he didn't leave me alone, good or bad, I'd have to mark up his pretty face. He stopped."

"You should have told me. I would have done a lot more than mark up his supposedly pretty face!"

Grady smiled.

"What are you smiling about?"

"It's just nice to have someone be so protective. You make me feel safe, Mitch. Among other things," he added in an undertone.

"You've already had one jerk in your life. You don't need to be bothered by another one."

"That's for sure."

"Just point me out in the audience tonight and mention your vicious bodyguard is out there."

"You're coming tonight?"

"Of course. I'm coming every night."

"But, Mitch, you'll get so bored."

"It's only seven more performances, so I only have seven more chances to see you work your magic."

"Mitch...."

"I need a drink," Mitch said, to avoid the awkward moment. He walked out of the room toward the kitchen. Grady followed him.

"It'll help, you know," Grady told him.

"What will?"

"Knowing you're in the audience. When someone important is there, it lifts the whole performance for me."

Important? Mitch smiled and promptly forgot what he'd come into the kitchen for.

"Aw, Grady, I'm no theater critic. As they say, I know what I like, but that's as far as it goes."

Grady walked over to Mitch, put his hands on Mitch's shoulders, looked into his eyes, and said, "There's important, and then there's *important*. Two different things."

Grady's look was so intent that Mitch was struck dumb for a moment. Speechless, he just stood there, hoping his inner trembling didn't show. After a time Grady gave him a puzzled look, dropped his arms, and stepped back.

"My... my first brush with plays," Mitch said desperately, anxious to start a new topic, "was when I took a course in college called 'French Literature in Translation.'"

He was relieved when he saw Grady smile and seem to relax.

"I thought it would be good for me to have a background in some of the classics," Mitch went on. "Little did I know that meant *Beowulf, Pantagruel,* Montaigne's essays, Balzac, and Stendhal. De Maupassant's short stories were terrific. But the great moment was at the end of the semester, when I was up on the roof getting some sun, and I started to read *Cyrano de Bergerac.* I didn't even remember where I was until I came to the end. So I guess I do know what I like. And I like seeing you do Iago."

"I'm a bit better than Beowulf?"

"Oh, my God, yes. There's not even anything to compare."

And so on Friday, Mitch set out for the theater with a highly charged Grady. When he insisted they take a cab, Grady argued that it would cost too much, but Mitch overruled him by telling him that it would be easier on his constitution to know that he'd gotten Grady safely to the theater in time for the sign-in. And besides, he wanted to get there early to get a front-row seat. Grady finally came around. Somehow, during the ride, their hands came together (Mitch figured Grady just needed grounding before a performance) and remained that way until the cab pulled up in front of the theater. Mitch was disappointed way out of proportion when they unclasped their hands.

There were already a few people at the box office when they stepped out.

"See?" Mitch said. "I do not want to sit way in the back. I want to be able to see all your facial expressions."

Grady went up to the box office, and, after saying hello to the girl in charge, asked that a ticket be set aside for Mitch for the next three performances that week and the four the next.

When she asked if Mitch was his agent, Grady replied, "Something like that."

"Your agent?" Mitch asked.

"Well, I could hardly say you're my... what... personal groupie!"

"It's only the truth."

"I'd better go and get ready."

"Oh, I forgot," Mitch said, "you have to 'prepare'... like Cassio."

"Right," Grady tossed over his shoulder as he hurried off.

Mitch remembered the conversation he'd had with Grady about the Method.

"The Method?" he'd asked Grady. "What's that?"

Each was sitting at his own end of the sofa, each with a pillow behind his back, lately returned from a little jaunt to the Tasti D-Lite, which featured an all-natural, low-calorie frozen yogurt-type dessert. Almost like ice cream. Naturally, they both had chosen chocolate.

"It started at the Moscow Art Theatre by a teacher named Stanislavski, who, incidentally, stated several years later that it was a process they'd tried, but had moved on to other things at that time, and he was amazed that it had become such an almost overpowering presence in the American theater."

Mitch was savoring every spoonful of his treat. Actually it was a sometime special called chocolate mousse, which had a thicker, creamier consistency than regular chocolate. He ate as slowly as possible as he was always so let down when he found himself scraping the bottom of the cup.

As Grady went on explaining, Mitch noticed that he too seemed to want to savor his dessert.

"The Method is more complicated than this, but one of the main precepts is the endowing of a character."

"What's endowing mean?" Mitch asked.

"Well, as Iago, if I were a Method actor, I'd have to endow— read: put in place of Othello—someone from my own past, say an evil uncle who was always horrible to me. And I'd keep seeing my imaginary uncle in place of Othello. The feelings of hate toward that uncle would supposedly convey from the stage."

"That seems like… I don't know… once removed, I guess."

"Generally speaking, they research their character and construct a whole life biography for them. It's notoriously difficult with Shakespeare because, not being royalty, we never had an uncle who even remotely lived like that, especially when it's a king."

"Sounds like a lot of extra work."

Grady laughed lightly. "I remember once I was in a play by Somerset Maugham called *The Breadwinner*, and its various scenes took place in Britain in 1908. This Method guy was so busy reading a history of England that he missed his entrance."

Mitch chuckled. "You know, it seems like I've read about some very famous actors who were 'Method.'"

"Oh sure—Marlon Brando, Shelley Winters, Rod Steiger, Maureen Stapleton."

"How about them? Aren't they considered great actors?"

"I always thought they were just naturally gifted. There's a famous story about the time Laurence Olivier and Dustin Hoffman were making *The Marathon Man*. Whether it's true or not, it's become the stuff of urban legend. Dustin Hoffman had a scene where he had to appear haggard and worn out, having stayed up all night, so he stayed up all night and ran around the block or the building and came dragging in to shoot the scene. When Laurence Olivier asked about his condition, he said, 'I've got this scene where I'm supposed to have been up all night, so I stayed up all night.' In all seriousness, Laurence Olivier asked, 'But, dear boy, wouldn't it have been easier to simply act it?'"

Mitch lost it and started laughing. Luckily, he'd finished his treat or there would have been chocolate mousse all over the sofa. Grady had to get up and pat him on the back, as he started choking. Grady gradually turned the pats into a gentle massage. Mitch had leaned into his strong hands, when it suddenly came to him that he was enjoying Grady's attention way too much. He stood as casually as he could and said, "I'd better put this cup in the trash before I really do spill it on something."

Grady let his hands slip down Mitch's back as Mitch hurried off.

Now, suddenly aware of the audience around him, awakening from his recollections with the same warm feelings he'd had then, Mitch realized he was sitting in his seat but didn't remember how he'd gotten there. Only now was he aware of the buzzing of the audience and the rustling of programs. Then, as he sat up straight, the house lights dimmed and the play began.

Just like the previous night, Mitch was totally mesmerized by the play from the moment Grady entered. Gone was the vaguely dusty odor of the theater, the rustle of the audience, and the slightly scratchy feel of the worn leather seats. He marveled from time to time at how his gentle Grady could become this despicable creature on the stage. He didn't notice that, quite obliviously, he referred to Grady as "his Grady."

When the house lights came up, causing Mitch to shade his eyes from what seemed to be sunlike brightness after the dim stage lighting, he was too emotionally exhausted to battle the crowds in the lobby.

He seemed unable to stop wondering about his mixed-up feelings for Grady. He had to admit that he awaited Grady's appearance when he returned from work or rehearsal. His apartment seemed so empty, so lifeless without the warmth Grady brought to his existence. Could he get along without it? Oh, he knew at some level that they would always be a major presence in each other's lives, but separately or together? And just what would "together" entail? His take on his emotions concerning Grady went back and forth like a tennis ball in a match at Wimbledon. The emotions Grady provoked in him were, he had to admit, more than friendship. But the big *L* word? At times he felt quite sure it was. At other times he simply couldn't go there; it was too much to handle. After all this time… no, he just couldn't bring himself to open that tightly closed door, the door that had kept back almost unbearable pain… kept it back, that is, until now.

His reverie was interrupted when the second act began; he hadn't even noticed the sound of the audience shuffling back into the theater. Then the play whisked him away again from his troublesome silent dialogue, actually a debate: Mitch against Mitch.

The play seemed to rush to its inevitable cathartic ending. Mitch joined the audience in applauding madly, even stinging his palms when Grady appeared.

Mitch hurried, as much as was possible, given the crush of people heading for the doors outside. He relished the cool night air on his face when he finally managed to get to the street. There was a pleasant, almost balmy, breeze brushing his cheeks that would have done a butterfly proud. He was looking down, trying to see patterns in the cracked sidewalk, when he heard his name called softly, in a voice that wasn't Grady's. He turned to see a young woman approaching him.

"Emilia," he said, finally recognizing the actress out of costume.

"Thank you, it's flattering to be remembered offstage, but my real name is Patty Ingram." She held out her hand. "That's Patty with a *Y* not Patti with an *I*. I'm not that pretentious."

Mitch took her slender hand in both of his in a gentle handshake.

"I hurried so I could meet you before Grady was finished."

"Oh…."

"Yes. I don't mean to overstep, but I wonder if you realize just how much Grady… ah… admires you?"

"Well—"

"He mentions you all the time—what you say, what your thoughts are on any subject. I've seen Grady in many situations, and I have to say I've never seen him so happy, so buoyant."

"Grady is a great guy."

"He is that. And he deserves much better than Hank. I disliked Hank so much it was difficult to be nice to him."

"I assume Grady told you what Hank did. I only wish justifiable homicide were possible. I think Grady was almost as shocked as he was hurt. I've never seen anyone so distraught."

"Grady and I have done several plays and workshops together, so we've become good friends. The last show we were in together, our dear Randall was part of the cast. Hank often used to come to performances and usually had some meaningless criticism for Grady. I wanted to slap him."

"I understand. I'd like to deck him, even now."

"Please don't repeat this, but when Grady turned our dear Randall down flatly and actually laughed at him, he settled on revenge by going after Hank. It didn't take much persuasion, from the flirting I saw going on between them. And then, of course, Hank suddenly stopped coming to rehearsals. Too busy elsewhere, I guess. He told Grady that he didn't want to spoil the performance by seeing the rehearsals too often. I wanted to say something to Grady, but I simply couldn't see him hurt that badly."

"He's heard about Hank's dalliances from a couple of other sources, but I won't add this story to the others. He feels he was stupid, which is so far from the truth. He just trusts other people are as sincere as he is."

"Yes. I think Grady thought what he and Hank had was 'love,' when the love involved was all his. He never knew there could be a truer love that wasn't so heavily one-sided. He didn't know anything else.

"Oh," she said suddenly, "here he comes. If you feel anything at all besides friendship for Grady, and from what I see, you do, please don't blow this."

"Hi, gang," Grady said. "Should my ears be buzzing?"

"Absolutely," Mitch replied, still fuzzy from Patty's last remark. "We were just fighting over who would be president and who would be vice president of the 'Grady's The Nicest Guy In The World' club. We finally had to settle on being cochairmen."

"You guys," Grady mumbled, looking up at the sky.

Patty kissed Grady on both cheeks, French style, and then, surprisingly, did the same to Mitch. And she was off, waving good-bye over her shoulder.

"She seems as nice as she is talented," Mitch observed.

"She's been a good friend to me. And acting opposite her in this show has been a real treat. She really helped me when she put Randall III in his place in front of the entire cast."

"Well, that makes her my friend for life. Come on, lo—laddie, let's go home."

He'd almost said, "come on, love." Did he mean "love" or was it just a figure of speech? He really had to be more careful until he could figure all this out. If he could, of course.

Mitch threw his arm across Grady's shoulder, and they started companionably down the street in search of a taxi.

"This must be the current 'commitment,'" said a mocking voice behind them.

Mitch stopped walking and turned around as Grady did likewise beside him. There was Randall with an arrogant smirk on his face.

"Right on, there, Randy," Mitch replied. "And…?"

"And, of course, I suppose your new partner is different from your old one," Randall said to Grady.

"What's that supposed to mean?" Grady said.

The nasty smile grew larger. "Well, at least he's mauling you instead of the other way around. Hank said many times how you were always all over him even though you were a tepid lover. That you guys made tepid love. Of course, I found him hot as hell."

Grady looked thunderstruck.

"You rotten son of a bitch," Mitch said after a guttural sound that did not sound human. "I'll kill you!" He started toward the other man, who ran away from them up the street. In his rage, Mitch didn't watch

107

his steps; he tripped over the uneven sidewalk and almost fell. That gave Randall time to jump into a passing cab and take off. Mitch ran after the cab, even though there was no chance he could catch it. Finally he stopped and stood shaking with the great surge of adrenaline. Grady ran up beside him.

"Mitch, he isn't worth it."

"If I see him again, I'll make him sorry he ever lived." Mitch felt his fists knot so tightly his fingernails bit into his palms.

Grady put his hands on Mitch's shoulders and turned him until they were face-to-face. He just stared into Mitch's eyes until Mitch finally relaxed. Then he put his hands on either side of Mitch's face.

"I don't want you to get mixed up in this. I'll take care of it. It means the world to me that you're so protective of me, but, please, Mitch, let me handle it. I've got to work with him for another week. We can't let the play fall apart because of two of the actors."

Mitch just stared into the beautiful blue eyes that held such affection that his throat closed; he was unable to speak.

"Please, Mitch."

After a time, Mitch nodded. As they walked on, he put his arm across Grady's shoulders once again. Whatever the reason, he couldn't stop the urge for physical contact. Hell with it, for the moment, he simply didn't care.

They caught a cab and went home.

GRADY CAUGHT the apartment door just before it slammed shut, after being given an exceedingly angry push from Mitch.

"That bastard," Mitch said. He pulled off his leather jacket and threw it on the sofa, as if it was at fault and he was handing out retribution.

"Mitch," Grady said, coming up behind him and putting his hands on Mitch's shoulders again. "Mitch, it's okay. He couldn't say anything to me to make things worse. It's beginning to look like there's no one in New York that Hank *hasn't* slept with."

Mitch chuckled as the tension left him. Grady always had that effect on him. He leaned back as Grady dug his thumbs into his shoulders, working out the knots there. As Mitch melted into the comforting touch, he found himself wanting to turn around and pull Grady into his arms. With great reluctance, he threw himself down on the sofa, and once there, toed off his shoes.

"Thanks, Grady. You're so good to me."

"As you are to me, Mitch." Grady's stare was intense.

"How are you going to handle working with that evil son of a bitch?"

"Just like I have been. I'll ignore him. I think he loves the attention, even if it's negative."

"He's really screwed up."

"Patty warned me about him from the start. But he can play nice very well, and it takes some time for the hateful side to show itself. In another show that the two of them were in together, he made a play for Patty's boyfriend at the time, even though the guy was totally straight. But at a party one night, when the boyfriend was already halfway drunk, our friend coaxed him into one of the bedrooms and proceeded to have him down more booze, straight from the bottle, yet, until he was barely conscious. The guy's zipper was down and Randall was fumbling around looking for the Golden Fleece when Patty burst in looking for her missing boyfriend. After much screaming and slapping, she got her boyfriend into a cab and home. But he finally broke up with her because he said she reminded him too much of what almost happened. He was totally freaked out."

"That guy is a menace. You should have let me rough him up. Maybe he'd think twice about causing trouble again."

"No. It was best we just let it go. Knowing him, he'd probably have pressed assault charges. But more important, he would, I'm sure, have been too banged up to continue in the play, and we've all worked too hard to let that happen."

"You're right, of course," Mitch said. "I really lost it when he tried deliberately to hurt you. You've been through so much, and you're such a good guy. I couldn't stand him trying to bring you down. I literally saw red."

After a long silence Grady said, "It's nice to know that someone cares that much about me."

"I do," Mitch said before he could stop himself.

The tension in the room felt almost solid, it was so strong. Just as Mitch started to rise from the sofa, the doorbell rang. It was Em's signal. Releasing a long-held breath, Mitch slid across the room, almost tripping when his toes slipped under the edge of the carpet again. He managed, barely, to right himself, and after throwing a sheepish glance back at Grady, he opened the door. Em and Sarah burst into the room, all smiles and giggles.

"What's so funny?" Mitch asked as he closed the door.

"Sit down, boys," Em said. "Have we got news for you."

"It's the best news in the world," Sarah added.

Mitch and Grady quickly sat side by side on the sofa.

"Okay," Grady said, "what's the big story?"

"You tell them," Em said to Sarah.

After a moment Sarah held out her hand and said, "We got married."

Em put her hand next to Sarah's and showed an identical ring. "We just got in the car and went to Massachusetts. I drove!" Em added.

Mitch and Grady rose as one being and rushed to hug the happy couple. Soon all four were a tangled mess of arms and legs as the hugs passed from one to another.

"We figured at our age we know our minds, and we wanted the formality," Em said. "Plus we're on the way to getting our one-thousand-plus rights that marriage brings."

"Who knows?" Sarah said wistfully. "Perhaps it won't be too long before gay marriage is legal here in New York."

"Never happen," Mitch said.

"If we ever get a governor again like Mario Cuomo, I'll bet we could," Em said.

"Yeah," Mitch agreed. "He was a good guy. If he was governor now, it just might be possible."

"Imagine Mario Cuomo getting put out of office by the mayor of Peekskill," Grady added. "I'm still shocked that that could happen."

"We would have had you two come with us," Sarah said, "but we knew Grady was busy with the play, and if we couldn't have both of you there, we decided we'd rather have a little private ceremony later. Just the four of us."

"We'll write our own vows," Em said.

"That's so sweet," Mitch said.

"Well, that's enough saccharine," Em stated. "Now that we've broken the ice, so to speak, maybe some other folks will be brave enough to follow suit."

"I've still got a bottle of champagne left from opening night," Mitch said quickly. "I think a toast is in order."

"Coward," Em whispered as Mitch passed her.

WHEN THE newlyweds had left, Mitch and Grady drifted over to the sofa, where Mitch took "his" end, facing the kitchen, and Grady took "his" end, facing the door. This was never planned; it just seemed to evolve. It was pure instinct, and Mitch wondered what strange power had caused the phenomenon. He hadn't come to any profound conclusion; it just seemed comfortable. Maybe there was a certain stability, a certain permanent feeling if they each had a designated "place." Mitch didn't realize he was running his finger along the welt on the sofa cushion, back and forth, back and forth until he suddenly became aware of the slight friction, and he slowed his hand until it just rested alongside his body. He noticed the lingering smell of roses. Sarah's perfume, he decided. She always seemed to smell of roses. It would never be Em. He'd given her a very expensive bottle of Coty's *Emeraude*, an old fragrance that had been Caroline's favorite. She'd chuckled, thanked him, and said she'd sniff it once in a while to remind her of Caro, but she'd never actually wear it.

"What did you think?" Grady asked.

"About what?" Mitch looked up to see an intense look on Grady's face.

"The recent nuptials, of course."

"Well, I guess it's really sweet. Pretty speedy, though."

Grady leaned over and pulled Mitch's feet into his lap. He took off Mitch's shoes and socks and began to massage his feet.

111

"As Em said, I guess they figured they shouldn't waste a lot of time at their age." As Grady spoke his hands stilled.

"Don't stop. That feels so good," Mitch said. Then he added, "I guess at any age, if you're sort of filled up and spilling over with... well, with... love, you want the world to know. Some sort of recognition. Some sort of ritual, a solemnity. Do you believe in gay marriage?"

"Sure I do. If you love someone, you want public recognition of that bond. And this second-class status is so horribly unfair. Separate but equal was proven false with Brown v. Board of Education. I suggested it to Hank several times, but his reaction was always, 'Why do we need to mimic straights? We know what we are. That's enough. Who needs a stupid piece of paper?'"

"And...?"

"I finally gave up. He obviously didn't want us to marry. He said he'd wait until it was legal in the whole country. I guess I was lucky. Just think—I'd have to get a gay divorce."

Mitch found if he squinted a bit he could make the cactus in the Ansel Adams photo on the wall look like it was resting on Grady's shoulder.

"What's with the strange look?"

"Oh, nothing," Mitch said. He was a bit embarrassed for his little optical fantasy. "It's just, if I squint, I can make that cactus in the photo seem like it's growing out of your shoulder."

Grady laughed. "Mitch, we're having a serious conversation. No distractions allowed."

"Okay."

"How about you, Mitch? Do you believe in gay marriage?"

"Sure I do... for others. I don't think I'm capable of that much trust in the fates—they're so vengeful." He looked up to see Grady's piercing blue eyes. "I can't go through the kind of loss I had with Jared."

"But, Mitch, we all face uncertainty. That's just the way life is."

"I understand that rationally, but emotionally I can't overcome my fear. Frankly, commitment scares me."

Mitch tried to pull his feet from Grady's grasp, but Grady held on tightly.

"The reason I'm confronting you isn't to make you uncomfortable. You're such a great guy. You deserve someone special in your life. Also, it's a huge loss to that other guy, not having you available."

"Grady, I...."

"Mitch, I don't think you realize just how amazing you are."

Mitch felt waves of embarrassment, delight, confusion, and doubt wash through him in a Doppler effect, ebbing and flowing in intensity.

"Grady, I just...."

"Okay, okay, the writer in you recognizes purple prose. I won't go on," he said. "But it's true," he added in a barely audible whisper.

After a prolonged silence, Mitch finally spoke. "What about you, Grady? Surely after your recent experience with Hank, you can't feel ready to find that 'someone special' you mention."

"You know, I think maybe I am. Looking back, I realize that what I thought was love was really the comfort of habit. I'd never known anything else, and I thought what I felt was what everyone felt."

"And now?"

"It was a pale imitation. I feel like a different person than the one who was committed to Hank. I was naïve, and he was very persuasive. When he told me we had it all, I believed him. I didn't know there was so much more out there."

Grady had stopped massaging Mitch's feet and was simply holding them in a gentle but firm grip. His piercing glance at Mitch had an obviously expectant look. Knowing he wasn't imagining it, Mitch felt the atmosphere suddenly turn electric. A shiver ran from Grady's grip on his feet up through his torso and seemed to blast right through his head and the ceiling and off into the universe. He was stunned. He felt that at any moment something momentous would happen, something irrevocable. In an instant all he felt was abject fear; it overwhelmed him. He forced himself up off the sofa and strode into the kitchen, where he leaned over the sink and tried to calm himself.

After a few minutes, Grady strolled into the kitchen.

"I'm sorry," he said quietly.

Mitch just shook his head, unable to respond. And, of course, he was undoubtedly projecting his own mixed-up feelings onto Grady. The lingering look had probably been no more than concern for a friend.

Grady went on, "I know our conversation must have reminded you of Jared." After a small silence, he said, "Well, enough of serious talk. Let's figure out a time to celebrate with Em and Sarah. We can't just act like nothing important happened. I know, how about a surprise party? They can recite their vows, and we can get white crepe paper, and those fold-out bells, and maybe some sort of sign. Or we could take them out to the Four Seasons, or somewhere real swanky. What do you think?"

Mitch was well aware of Grady's motives. He was letting Mitch off the hook. Realizing how uncomfortable Mitch had become, he was trying to get beyond that awkward and scary moment, and back to the usual byplay between them. He took a deep breath.

Coward! Wimp! What was he afraid to face? Grady had almost admitted his feelings for Mitch. And he'd finally realized he had serious feelings for Grady. Why was that so terrifying? Grady was one in a million; Mitch should grab him and hold on for dear life.

Finally feeling more composed, he turned around, wanting to get past this strangeness.

"I… I think… I think we should celebrate here. Let's keep it a family affair," he managed in what he hoped was his normal voice. "Of course, we'll have to trick Em into dressing up again."

"We'll think of something."

"Well," Mitch said. "I'm beat. I think I'll turn in."

"Okay, me too," Grady said, turning and leaving the kitchen.

Had Grady's shoulders seemed to slump?

Idiot! This had been the perfect opportunity to declare himself. He knew exactly what he felt for Grady. It was love. That's what it was. He was just tied up by old fears. Somehow, he had to get over this before it was too late and Grady gave up on him. *Can't let that happen. God, no!*

Chapter Seven

THE FIRST week of performances of *Othello* seemed to Mitch to rush by like a theatrical comet. Although he went to every performance, it always seemed that he was seeing Grady's performance for the first time. He noticed little additions or alterations, making for an even richer performance, as the two nights fled past.

Grady had explained to him that this was likely to happen. He'd told Mitch that usually during the run of a play, the characters seemed to evolve of their own accord, and little nuances crept in as each actor became even more comfortable in his character. And there was the cumulative effect of this happening to all the actors on the stage, each reflecting off the others. He was fascinated. The only one who seemed frozen in exactly the same portrayal was his archenemy, Randall. Could he be prejudiced? Of course, but he didn't think so; he tried to compare all the other actors with Randall, and they seemed minutely changed as well. Mitch felt much satisfaction. On Saturday, just as they were leaving for the theater, a UPS guy arrived with a package for Grady. It turned out to be the script, copies of his costume sketches, and music for his songs in *Carousel*.

"You know," Grady said, "I don't know whether to be elated or scared to death."

"What do you mean?"

"Well, I've got to have this all down pat in one week."

"But look how fast you got Iago, and that's a much bigger part."

"Oh, it's not the text," Grady said. "It's the music. I can sing, but I've always found music much harder to learn. I'll have to find a piano player somehow."

"Wait. I think Em told me once that Sarah plays the piano."

"But this is the orchestra score, so there aren't any guitar chords. You have to play it as written."

"What do you mean, 'guitar chords'? I don't think Sarah plays the guitar."

"No, Mitch, guitar chords are those little notations—like Bm6 or A7—you see above the staff. That's what most pianists use to form the base. They don't read the accompaniment as written. They find it way too simple. Boring, in fact."

"Oh, okay. I also think Em said that Sarah even taught singing privately for many years. So she must be pretty good."

"We can ask, I guess. Wouldn't hurt."

"When we get home, I'll go down and ask her. I picked up a sack of birdseed for Tweet the other day, so we can deliver that at the same time."

"Perfect. Oh my God, it's late. We'd better get going."

For Mitch the show was as riveting as it had been on opening night. He was still in a bit of a daze when the two of them came through the front door of the apartment after the performance.

"We'd better go down to Em's before it gets too late. Unfortunately, she's a morning person, unlike us artiste types, so she usually goes to bed early."

"You go ahead," Grady said. "I always feel grubby after a show, like I didn't get all the makeup off. I only feel comfortable after I take a shower."

"Okay. I hope I'll be the bearer of good news."

"I'll concentrate on positive thoughts."

Mitch laughed as he went in the kitchen to get the birdseed. When he returned seconds later, he was carrying a huge sack.

As Grady pulled off his makeup-stained T-shirt, Mitch nearly dropped the birdseed. The man had almost no body fat; every muscle was sculpted to perfection. Mitch hadn't expected to be treated to this sight at that moment, and he was startled by his visceral reaction.

"Mitch," Grady said, "that's enough birdseed for a flock of eagles!"

"I… I know. But Em's always running out, so I thought I'd stock up for her."

"Hope she has somewhere to put it." Grady started toward the bathroom, and Mitch stood frozen as he watched that glorious V-shaped back disappear into the other room. He was relieved when Grady didn't turn back to see him absolutely transported.

He shook himself and quickly left the apartment.

Still a bit fuzzed, he nearly fell as he hurried down the stairs to Em's apartment. He envisioned the staircase covered in birdseed, could almost see the little black and gold seeds sprinkled everywhere, and was thankful for his quick reflexes. He managed to thump on the door with his knee, and soon he found Sarah peering around the door.

"Mitch," she said with a big smile. "Do come in. Emma's in the kitchen fixing us some tea. Will you join us?"

When Mitch was inside, Sarah closed the door and called out, "Emma, Mitch is here. I hope you're fixing chamomile—I know it's his favorite. He always has it on hand, along with peanuts."

They exchanged a knowing smile.

"What in the world have you got there?" Em said as she entered the room, holding a tray with a teapot under a cozy and three cups and saucers. They rattled ominously as she started laughing. "Tweet's only one little bird."

"Well," Mitch said, feeling sheepish, "I thought I'd help you stock up, and—"

"Hi, Mitch," Tweet screeched, saving Mitch from more embarrassment. "Hi, Mitch. He's a keeper. Hi, Mitch. Hi, Grady."

Mitch put the birdseed in the copper firewood holder at the side of the fireplace as the two ladies sat, Sarah in the chair and Em on the footstool at her feet.

"'Hi, Grady'?" he asked. "You taught him something new?"

"It was actually Sarah who did it. I think I've heard that phrase about ten thousand times in the last week."

Sarah blushed prettily, saying, "I wanted to thank him for that lovely performance. I hope he won't mind."

"Mind?" Mitch said. "He'll be absolutely delighted. He and Tweet have some sort of weird connection, so it's only right that they can call each other by name."

Mitch sat cross-legged on the Oriental rug and leaned back against the embroidered fire screen.

"Ah, Em, the perfect cup of tea, as usual. I can never make it quite like you do."

"I make a good cup of tea, if I do say so myself," Em replied.

Sarah, ever the diplomat, said, "I think you both make a delightful cup of tea."

Mitch sat up and set his cup on the stone hearth.

"I came down to ask you something as well as to deliver Tweet's lunch. Grady got the stuff from the theater upstate, and he's got to learn some music along with the text. I think I remember Em telling me you play the piano, Sarah. Do you think you could help him learn his music?"

"Oh, I'm not sure...."

"Of course she can," Em said. "She plays beautifully. She studied music for a long time. She wanted to be a concert pianist, for heaven's sake. She coached singing students. Opera. Of course, she can play for Grady."

"But, Emma," Sarah said, "I play classical music, I don't know if I have... what do they call it... the 'touch' for musical comedy."

"You played all the music from *Kismet* for me one time."

"But that's based on music by Alexander Borodin, so I already knew the melody and the tempos."

"I don't mean to put you on the spot," Mitch said.

"You're not putting Sarah on the spot," Em added. "The woman can play anything."

"But—"

"I know you can do it," Em said with finality.

"If it's all right with you, Sarah, I'll bring the music, and we could go over to your house tomorrow, and you could take a crack at it."

"Maybe soon you'll come to live with me 24-7," Em said.

"Oh, Emma," Sarah began, "I know how hard it is...."

"No, dear," Em said, "don't apologize. We agreed we'd take this slow, and I can certainly wait until you're completely comfortable staying with me all the time."

Mitch stared at Em with wonder. He'd never heard her voice sound so gentle, so tender. When Em looked at him, he nodded in appreciation. She nodded back.

After a moment Sarah said, "If Grady hears me and I sound horrible, I'll be so embarrassed."

"Grady will be busy learning his lines. It'll just be the three of us," Mitch said.

"Good. That's settled. We'll take the car. I'll drive," Em said in a firm voice that brooked no nonsense.

"If you drive, it won't matter if Sarah can play the music or not, because we'll all be dead!"

"Get out of here, you wretch. Before I stuff that birdseed down your throat!"

"Toughie," Mitch said as he stood up.

"She acts that way on purpose. She's really a gentle soul," Sarah said.

"Quiet, you'll ruin my reputation."

As Mitch hurried toward the door, he threw back over his shoulder, "That gentle soul can actually lacerate you with words."

"Hi, Mitch. Hi, Grady. He's a keeper!" Tweet screeched, getting in the last word.

WHEN MITCH got back to the apartment, he heard the music before he opened the door. On entering he found Grady lying on the sofa with a dreamy look in his eyes, listening to what had to be a recording of *Carousel.* Even he, not really a musical-comedy buff, recognized "June Is Busting Out All Over." He stood for a long moment enjoying the look of contentment on Grady's face. He was continually surprised at how expressive Grady was. Or was Grady just so intensely focused?

Grady looked up, and their gazes locked for an instant, much like two laser beams suddenly pointed directly at each other.

Or was he imagining this because he wanted it to be so? Maybe it wasn't a signal that they had similar feelings; maybe it was a look of "don't put me in an impossible situation." *Stop acting like a Libra— thinking one way, then the exact opposite,* Mitch thought.

Mitch looked away and sat in one of the chairs facing the sofa. He noticed for the first time that the predominant color in the Oriental rug was gold. He wondered why he was noticing such a thing at this particular time. Avoiding the subject?

"Good news, I hope?" Grady said.

"Ah, yeah. It turns out that Sarah studied music for a long time. She had dreams of becoming a concert pianist. She's afraid she can't 'do' musical comedy, but Em was, as is her way, quite vocal that she could. So while you're studying your lines tomorrow, we're going over to Sarah's house in Hoboken and give it a try."

"So you guys get to have all the fun, and I have to slave away learning lines."

"Didn't you quote me a line from some play about how much fun it was learning lines?"

"One of the characters, an actress named Irina Arkadina, says the line in Chekov's *The Seagull*: 'Ah, but how much better to be in one's hotel room learning a part.'"

"There you go."

"Some friend you are, turning my own words against me."

"Grady, I was only…."

"Oh, Mitch, listen. It's Billy and Julie's duet. I think this is one of the greatest love songs ever written: 'If I Loved You.'"

Grady had explained to Mitch that the song was about Billy and Julie being in love but also being afraid to actually say it. So they sing about how they would feel if they were in love. If I loved you I'd feel this or that. The irony was what made the song so moving, Grady had told him.

Mitch was suddenly swamped in the music. Overwhelmed. He felt elated and at the same time like he was drowning. The song was him. It was Grady and him. But should he acknowledge it? What if only he felt that way? What if he said something and lost the friendship that had become so essential to him?

Mitch felt the music brushing his skin, raising chills, much like a light touch of velvet. His attention remained riveted on the rug.

He heard the phrase about golden chances passing by. The words ran around in his mind like errant marbles. It seemed he could almost feel them bounding off the inside of his skull. Was he allowing a golden chance with Grady to pass him by?

Golden chances. Golden rug. Golden chances. Everything seemed golden. Passing him by. Golden chances passing him by.

As the music came to an end, the silence was almost a solid thing, like a block of cement. Mitch couldn't take it. He stood and rushed into the bathroom, slamming the door behind him. He looked at his face in the dimness of the night-light. He looked... haunted. He didn't know whether to laugh or cry. He felt that at any moment he could do either.

"Mitch?" came Grady's voice from the other side of the door. "Are you okay?"

He turned the water on, pretending he hadn't heard. These horrible thoughts about loss, about losing Jared, brought Mitch's worst fears right to the front of his mind. He simply couldn't let himself care that much about anyone ever again. He cupped handfuls of cold water over his face, splashing the basin and the floor. When he finally heard Grady knocking again, at first he tried not to notice.

"Mitch, please."

This was ridiculous—he had to get hold of himself. He wiped his face roughly on a towel, took a deep breath, and opened the door.

Grady took a step back. "I'm sorry. I'm so sorry."

"You... you're sorry? What for? I'm the one who should be sorry. Sorry for making a scene."

"I didn't realize that song might make you think of Jared. I just wasn't thinking."

"Jared?" Mitch said. "But it wasn't Jared. It was...."

"Come on," Grady said, taking him by the arm. "Time for a big dose of chocolate. Everything is better with chocolate."

Mitch let himself be led into the kitchen. Grady sat him at the table. When Grady turned the lights on, everything seemed so bright. He ran his hands through his hair and willed himself to calm down. In a moment Grady was back with a huge hunk of chocolate for each of them.

"Chocolate is good," Grady said, biting off a chunk.

Mitch did the same and let the luscious flavor slip down his throat. He felt better. Finally, he looked up sheepishly at Grady.

"Better?" Grady asked, patting Mitch's hand where it rested on the table.

"Much better," he answered.

That was all it took. His touch. He was sunk!

DURING THE ride down Seventh Avenue, Mitch didn't have time to think about much as Em, in her usual go-get-'em way was barreling along, threatening even the jaded cab drivers into fearful avoidance. With Em at the wheel of the Dodge, Sarah beside her, and Mitch careening around in the backseat, the trip was much like the bumper-car ride at the amusement park, except there were no actual bumps. For that, Mitch would be eternally grateful. He envied Grady, safely at home, learning lines.

"Slow down!" he'd hollered several times. "You're going to get us killed!"

Em merely laughed, stepped on the gas, and replied, "I want to get this show on the road."

"On the road, like roadkill?"

"I think Emma is a wonderful driver," Sarah said loyally, though her hat was tilted at a very odd angle. However she didn't seem frightened in the least.

Fortunately Em had to slow down as Seventh Avenue (Mitch always wondered at the reasoning) turned into Varick Street. Traffic began backing up as they neared the approach to the Holland Tunnel.

Two blocks away from the actual entrance to the tunnel, they went through four stoplight changes, each causing Em's frustration level to rise higher until it was a palpable presence in the car. Sarah, already used to Em's rather tempestuous nature, tried to "calm the waters" by telling them a little bit about Hoboken.

"You know," she started, "there's a very funny story about Hoboken. I don't know if it's true or not, but I always found it amusing. Do you know who Hermione Gingold is?"

"Wasn't she the one," Em replied through rather gritted teeth, "who sang 'I Remember It Well' with Maurice Chevalier in that movie with Leslie Caron? *Fifi*, or *Dede* or something?"

"*Gigi*," Sarah said.

"She was a kick," Em put in. "I remember watching her on talk shows. Very upper-class British, and very funny."

"That's the one," Sarah went on. "The story goes that a little theater in Hoboken was doing a revival of Sondheim's *A Little Night Music*. She played the grandmother in the Broadway production… and on a lark, the cast called her on the phone and asked her if she'd like to come to their performance in Hoboken." She was silent for a moment.

"And…?" Em asked, impatient as always.

"Well, she said, 'Darlings, I'd love to come.' And after a pause, 'Where *is* Hoboken?'"

They all laughed, Mitch as much because they'd finally reached the approach's curve leading right into the tunnel itself. Of course, they had to merge with the traffic coming from another approach on their left. The traffic oozed like thick maple syrup into two lanes and then whooshed into the tunnel.

"I remember seeing a movie one time about an explosion here in the tunnel, and the water was roaring in," Mitch said. "Every time I go through here, I get just a little worried."

"Scaredy-cat," Em noted.

"Now, Emma," Sarah soothed.

Sparkling pure white tiles and flashing red reflections flew by Mitch's field of vision as he once again hung on for dear life. It seemed the other drivers had fallen prey to Em's speed-demon tendencies. As they flew out the other end of the tunnel, Mitch heaved a gigantic sigh, looking forward to a relatively slower ride through the streets of Hoboken.

Mitch was totally enchanted by Hoboken. As they drove along, he saw brownstones on the right and little stores on the left. As they passed by, Mitch saw a long line, almost a block long, in front of one of the stores. It had a pink-and-white awning over the front of the building, which was constructed of warm pinkish bricks.

"What's that?" he asked. "It looks like the line for a sold-out movie... but no theater."

"It's a bakery," Sarah said.

"A bakery," Mitch parroted. "With a line like that?"

"Carlo's Bake Shop," Sarah told him. "There since 1910. It's very famous. They make absolutely fantastic cakes. Really, more like works of art."

Just then, a man with a chef's white hat stuck his head out of the upper story window. The crowd broke into applause, and camera flashes ricocheted off the building's front.

"He's quite famous. He's called the Cake Boss," Sarah said.

"Hmmm," Em added. "Just like the Soup Nazi."

That got a laugh from all three, as it would from any *Seinfeld* fan. As they drove along, Sarah, now their tour guide, kept up a running commentary on the passing scene.

"We've gotten very refined these days," Sarah said. "See that little bar on the left, S. Sullivan's?"

"Yes," Mitch said.

"That used to be called Stinky Sullivan's years ago."

"Sarah!" Em said.

"What?"

"It sounds so funny hearing such a word coming out of your mouth."

"Never mind."

"I think it's a good thing," Em said rather smugly.

"Don't worry, Em's attitude reflects off everyone she comes in contact with," Mitch said.

And with that said, they continued down Washington Street.

"Turn right here on Seventh," Sarah said.

Looming before them was the massive Stevens Institute of Technology, a most impressive building, Mitch thought. At Sarah's direction, they turned right again and continued along Hudson Street for one block.

"This is it," Sarah said, indicating another right. "The little red brick one. You can pull around in the back. There's parking in the alley."

Mitch thought it was a charming little house, the front oddly perpendicular to Hudson Street, where they'd just turned. As they passed along its side, Mitch noted a gabled roof, black wrought iron fence and stairway, and what seemed to be a large planted area—lawn and flowers fronting the house. A high, sheltering hedge behind the fence blocked a clear view. As they swung around the building, there was, indeed, a cobblestone alley. Em brought them to a bone-shuddering stop in a parking area, separating them from the house next door.

Mitch was delighted to feel solid ground under his feet. He tried not to think of the first part of the ride, the part before they actually reached Hoboken, as it was one of blaring horns and images of other cars being passed in such proximity he could distinguish minute scratches in their paint.

Mitch took in the exceptionally wide terra-cotta painted garage doors beneath a strange half circle of bricks above.

"This was originally a coach house, and that blocked-up half circle was the hayloft," Sarah told Mitch after seeing his puzzled look. "The wide doors were for their carriages."

Sarah led them back along the street, through the gate, across the lawn on ladybug-shaped stepping-stones, and on into the house.

Once inside Mitch felt his feet sink into a very lush wall-to-wall carpet in dark green. All the matching furniture, living room and dining room, was mahogany traditional. A large seascape dominated one side of the room, across from which was a baby grand piano, again in mahogany. A Spanish shawl draped from its lid; atop the shawl was a cut glass vase holding an array of pink silk roses.

"What a beautiful room," Mitch remarked.

"But kind of boring," Sarah said, "don't you think?"

"Oh my God," Mitch said. "The Em influence. You've gone all bohemian."

"And there's no Tweet," Em said.

"Peaceful," Mitch replied.

"I'm going to report your attitude to Tweet, and he'll bite you in revenge."

"No, he's not as bloodthirsty as some people I know."

"How sharper than a serpent's tooth," Em quoted.

"You win. How can I top one of King Lear's lines?"

"This was my husband's taste," Sarah said. "I've always thought it looked a little like a setting in a furniture store."

Though it was undoubtedly a beautiful room, Mitch sort of agreed with her, but he didn't say so.

Sarah walked over to the piano and raised the lid from the keys. She ran a finger over them, causing a little cascade of music. Mitch took the piano score over to her and placed it on the rest. Sarah stretched her fingers, opened the score to the overture, sat down, and proceeded to play it flawlessly.

When she finished Mitch realized his jaw had dropped open, much like a cartoon figure showing amazement. For once even Em was speechless. After a bit Sarah said, "I hope I got the tempo right. I've never played much musical comedy."

"It was perfect!" Em gushed.

"It was," Mitch added. "I listened to the CD last night, and the tempo was exactly the same. You even got that merry-go-round feeling just right."

"Well, I suppose that makes me dear Grady's accompanist," Sarah said.

"That it does," Mitch told her. "Thank heavens. What a relief. Now let's go back and tell him the good news."

"Except he'll have to come all the way over here. You have no piano," Em said to Mitch.

"I've already figured that out. I'll take care of it on the way back. Oh," he added, "I'm driving. No arguments. You may have the sharpest tongue, but I'm bigger."

"We'll sit in the back and make out," Em said.

"Oh, Emma," Sarah said, blushing as pink as the roses on the piano. "You are so bad."

"Always," Mitch agreed.

And on that note they rushed to the car.

GRADY WAS rehearsing his lines when they returned. Sarah, using Mitch's keys, opened the door, and after stepping inside, she held it for the other two. Em followed with a strange-looking contraption under her arm, and Mitch followed her, struggling with something long and narrow, wrapped in some kind of blanket. Once they were all inside, Sarah closed the door and said, "We're back."

"What the hell…," Grady began.

"All will be revealed to you in a minute," Mitch said in a portentous voice as he placed his bundle carefully on the sofa.

Em set up her strange contraption, which resembled a large black luggage rack.

"Close your eyes," Sarah said excitedly.

Grady tried again. "Mitch—"

"You have to close your eyes," Em said in her most commanding voice. Grady's eyes snapped shut.

Mitch unwrapped his burden and placed it on the black stand.

"Okay," the three of them squealed.

Grady opened his eyes and turned to see a Yamaha keyboard sitting in the middle of the living room. He looked from the keyboard to each of the others without a word.

Breaking the long silence, Mitch said, "Sarah plays the piano just like she was born in the pit at a musical. She sight-read the overture perfectly."

"I'm going to be your accompanist."

"But… but…."

"No buts, my friend," Mitch said. "We want you to do us proud when you start your first rehearsal. I rented it for a solid week. Do you think you can do it in a week? I mean, there's all those chorus bits you have to sing as well as 'When The Children Are Asleep.'"

"Oh, I can learn all of it in a week, but, Mitch, you've already done too much for me. I don't want—"

"Not another word," Mitch said, crossing to Grady and then putting his hand over Grady's mouth.

127

Mistake! Oh, God, his lips! They were positively luscious. He quickly dropped his hand and stepped back.

"Come on, Sarah," he managed. "Let's show Grady how beautifully you play."

Sarah took off her hat, placed it carefully on the table next to the sofa, and crossed to the keyboard with a look on her face that stated in a nice way, "I can't reach the keys from the floor." Mitch hastily ran to the kitchen and ran back with a kitchen chair.

Sarah thanked him as he secured the plastic music rest to the keyboard as Em quickly placed the piano score on it. Once again Sarah stretched her fingers before sitting down. Mitch knelt and straightened the rug, which had become rumpled, preventing the pedal attachment from lying flat. As he stood up, Sarah began to play.

Once again the haunting overture to *Carousel* filled the room. The three stood entranced. She had only gotten to the second page when they heard Mitch's doorbell.

"Who could that be?" Em said. "We're all here."

Grady hurried to the door and looked through the peephole.

"It's Hank!"

Em grabbed Grady's hand and dragged him off toward the back bedroom.

"You two deal with him. I'll get our treasure out of sight," she called over her shoulder.

After he was sure they'd disappeared, Mitch opened the door.

"Can I help you?"

"Yes," the other man said in a friendly voice. Mitch noticed, with great satisfaction, that he was at least two inches taller than Hank. "I'm looking for a dear friend of mine. Grady Gilmore. I understand he may be staying here with you."

"Grady Gilmore. How alliterative."

"Is he here?"

"As you can see, my friend Sarah and I were just enjoying a little musical interlude, which we'd really like to get back to. Right, Sarah?"

"Yes," Sarah said, and added in a firm voice. "You've made me lose my place. Now I'll have to start over." She rose and joined Mitch at the door. Being tall, Sarah could look rather intimidating at times. She did now.

"So, he's not here."

"I think I've heard a name like that somewhere around the neighborhood," Mitch admitted. "That's what I can tell you. Now, we must get back to our music."

"But…."

"Sorry," Sarah said as Mitch closed the door.

"And the two of us were having such a good time," Mitch said loud enough for his words to carry through the door. He figured that was the truth, they were… along with the other two. So he wasn't really lying.

Overactive conscience; lying to a liar was okay even if he did lie, which he hadn't. After checking through the peephole, he said softly, "You can come out now."

Em appeared first, Grady behind her. He was smiling broadly, and Em gave a thumbs-up.

"Let's just go on as if nothing happened," Mitch stated. "Let's not let old Hank spoil our fun."

"Good idea," Grady said.

"Well," Em said, sitting on the arm of the chair next to the keyboard, "let's hear the two of you together."

Mitch sat in the chair beside her. "We're sitting down so we can't pass out from delight."

"I doubt that'll happen," Grady answered.

He stood next to the keyboard, and Sarah looked up at him, smiled, and nodded. At his signal, she began the introduction to "When The Children Are Asleep." When the time came for Grady to join in, his rich high baritone filled the room. Both Mitch and Em looked at him with wonder. Then they looked at each other, and Mitch's broad smile was reflected by Em's.

"I knew it," Mitch whispered. "He's really good."

"I never doubted it. I've heard him a few times singing softly to Tweet."

As Grady sang, Mitch found his rush of emotions hard to decipher: admiration, pride, wonder, and… and a tingling warmth. It was certainly more than affection, more in the category known all over the world as…. He forced his mind to concentrate on the heavenly sounds filling the room.

After Sarah played the last few chords and stopped, the silence was absolute. Then Em stood up and began to applaud. Mitch stood too, strode over to Grady, and placed a hand on each of his shoulders.

"Grady," he said seriously, "that was… I don't know what the right word would be."

"Try splendiferous," Em supplied.

"Overwhelming," Mitch finally uttered. "I was transported. You are so talented."

Grady blushed charmingly. "Oh, Mitch, thanks, but I think you're just a bit biased."

"I probably am. But at the same time, when I can't find the right words, you know my reaction isn't just plain approval."

Grady looked into Mitch's eyes. "I do."

They stood like that for a time, until Em said, "Can I get a word in too?"

Mitch lowered his arms and turned, suddenly aware again that there were others in the room.

"Sure. Your turn."

"It was truly beautiful. But you have to give credit to the fine accompaniment."

"Oh, Sarah," Mitch blurted, "I'm so sorry. You were fantastic too. I guess it's just that I heard you play so perfectly at your place, and this is the first time I've heard Grady sing."

"Not to worry," Sarah said. "The best thing you can say to an accompanist is that you never noticed the music, only the singer."

"Well, I did," Em said.

"As Grady just said, you might be just a bit biased."

"I sure am, and I'm proud of it."

Before the congratulations could go any further, the phone rang.

Mitch crossed and picked up the phone. After listening for a moment, he turned to the others. "It's Brandon, and he sounds horribly upset."

Startled looks flew between all four of them.

"What?" Mitch said. "Slow down, I can't understand you." He turned to the others. "He's crying so hard I can't make out a word."

He sat on the edge of his desk and pressed the phone to his ear, as if that could help him hear better. He tried to speak several times but gave it up as useless. In frustration, he took the phone away from his ear and gave it several abrupt shakes, as if he were shaking a reluctant bottle of catsup. This wasn't the supposedly "cured" Brandon. This was more like the Brandon who'd been his confidant so many years ago.

"Stop," he almost shouted. "Brandon. Brandon! I said stop! Do you remember my address?" He paused. "Okay. Repeat it. Good. Now what I want you to do is get in a cab and come over here. Right now. I'll be waiting for you, and we can hash all this out together. Okay?"

Mitch dropped the phone and looked at the others, feeling confused. Their concerned looks only intensified his own feelings. This was his family. His little family. And Mitch realized they were concerned because they sensed his own feelings, as he knew closely knit family units were wont to do. His apartment, with its strangely compatible mix of furnishings seemed to become a soft and perfect background for its inhabitants. His emotions were a jumble, children's blocks tumbling from a too-tall tower. Mixed in with the worrisome thoughts about his old friend, who'd sounded almost at the brink of madness, was overwhelming affection for the three others in the room. Then, when his glance settled on Grady, he felt waves of love take possession of him. There wasn't a speck of doubt left. He'd fallen in love, deeply in love, for a second time; something he'd thought was impossible.

"Did you get any idea of what was wrong?" Grady asked, breaking his mood.

"Not really. He was incoherent. He was hysterical, almost out of it."

"Something dreadful must have happened," Sarah offered. She ran her hands over the keyboard in a nervous little crescendo. "I had a student once who got a phone call that turned out to be a message that his older brother had been hit by a car and was on the way to the hospital. He started screaming, and I couldn't get him to stop. It was terrifying to see someone so upset."

"What did you do?" Em asked.

"Well, finally, I just took him in my arms and squeezed him really hard, and I kept saying over and over that it would be okay. He went limp in my arms, and soon his father came to pick him up. By then he'd calmed down, and I never said anything to the father. I didn't want to embarrass him."

"You may have to squeeze Brandon," Em said. "Really hard."

Nervous chuckles followed. This, however, seemed to break the stricken atmosphere. Em and Sarah went off to the kitchen, saying that tea might be needed, just in case.

"I'm feeling sort of guilty," Mitch said.

"My God, why?" Grady said.

"I've been so mean to Brandon lately."

Grady crossed the room and took Mitch in his arms. At once, Mitch felt the tension leave him as he warmed to the comforting touch. He felt strong hands soothing his back, alternating with little pats. They always seemed to be standing so close, with one's hands on the other's shoulders, almost, but not quite, a real embrace. Like they simply needed to touch, to comfort.

"He was acting like an ass, and he deserved to be treated like one. The fact that he's in distress now doesn't change that. What I think is important is that, without even thinking twice, you told him to come to you. All the badgering and insults were forgotten, and you only wanted to ease his pain. Don't beat up on yourself."

Mitch leaned back and looked into the blue eyes opposite him. "Thanks, Grady. That helps a lot. You're so good for me."

Suddenly feeling awkward, Mitch gave him a hug and stepped back, as Em and Sarah came in from the kitchen with the tea in a pot and mugs on a tray, which they set on the end table on a kitchen towel they'd brought along. It wasn't long before the doorbell rang, and they heard a scratching noise at the door.

Mitch crossed quickly and opened the door. Brandon fell into the room, his blotchy red face a mass of tears, his nose running, his clothes rumpled and dirty, his bow tie gone, his hair matted, and no suitcase.

"I'm—I'm going—to hell," he cried. "To hell... and I should. Oh God, what... what am I going to do?"

Mitch leaned over and put a hand under each of Brandon's arms, then drew him up off the floor.

"Brandon," he said, "try to calm down. Tell me what's wrong. What happened?"

"Oh, Mitch! I—I've been so mean to you. You should kick me out. You... somebody should just... just kill me. I'm a rotten mess, and I'm going to hell."

Mitch felt a tugging at his shirt and turned to see Sarah behind him.

"Let me," she said, and taking Mitch's place, she pulled Brandon to her in a fierce embrace. "Now you just stop it," she commanded, ever the stern singing teacher, the one feared by all. She had a towel in her hand. She pulled back and began to wipe his face. He seemed to relax a bit.

"That's it, dear," she said in a calm, controlled voice with almost a purr in it. "You just let me fix your face and then you must have a cup of tea and tell us what's wrong."

Brandon whimpered, but Sarah just continued to clean up his face.

"Now stop," she said. "You're doing just fine." She smoothed his hair, straightened his coat, and brushed the lapels briskly. Brandon watched her, seemingly hypnotized by her calm demeanor and soothing words. He put his head on her shoulder and heaved a great sigh. She patted his back, pulled him over to the sofa, and sat down with him. Em brought over a mug of tea, which Sarah took from her and held to Brandon's lips, coaxing him into taking a few sips. She held the mug away for a moment and then had him drink again. And she kept doing so until the entire mug was empty.

The others watched with great fascination as this little saga progressed. Mitch thought of the article he'd read once about how a mongoose could mesmerize a snake, although it wasn't really nice to compare Sarah to a mongoose.

"There now," Sarah said. "That's better. I always say there's nothing like a cup of tea to make everything just a little bit better."

Mitch was surprised but amused at the same time at the way this quiet, shy woman had taken charge and turned what could have been a very messy situation into a counseling session. People always amazed him with the different facets of their personalities, sometimes at odds with each other.

Now, in a strangled voice, Brandon said, "I've sinned. Oh, Mitch, I've sinned, and I'm going to hell."

Mitch sat on the chair opposite Brandon and Sarah.

"You're not going to hell. Please, just tell us what happened." He leaned forward, his elbows on his knees. Grady sat on the arm of the chair, as if to give Mitch moral support. Em sat on the kitchen chair near the keyboard. Mitch was relieved because now no one seemed to be looming over Brandon.

"I was at the bus station," Brandon began so softly they could barely hear him. "And this guy sat down next to me, and we started talking. And it was nice and friendly. I guess he noticed that I was reading my Bible, because he started talking about the Psalms, and which was his favorite."

"A born-again?" Mitch asked.

"I guess so. I never asked. But he certainly knew the Psalms. He quoted some of the lines. Anyway, when I had to go to the men's room, I asked him to watch my suitcase, and he said okay."

"He stole your suitcase?" Mitch asked.

"No. I only wish it was as simple as that. When I was washing my hands, he snuck into the men's room behind me and started kissing my neck. I was so surprised that I didn't do anything. It felt so good to be close to someone. I hadn't in so long. Then when I realized what was happening, I pushed back and turned around. Before I could stop him, he took hold and started kissing me on the mouth. I started to fight him, but then something seemed to come over me, and I was kissing him back."

It seemed to Mitch that Brandon forgot where he was as he relived in his mind the incident he was describing. Without knowing, a small smile took possession of his lips, and his voice grew softer.

"We were rubbing against each other and pressing like mad, and then… and then… then…."

"I think we can guess the rest," Mitch said, aware that the ladies were present, which made him uncomfortable, whether it did the same to them or not. Beside him, he heard Grady suppress a chuckle.

"But, Mitch," he said, the smile gone, anguish taking hold of his face. "I liked it... I liked it. After all my teachings, I liked it!"

"Well, of course you did," Mitch said. "You've been brainwashed by a bunch of bigots. Brandon, my God, face it: you're gay. You like men just like I do. Like Grady here does. We're born this way. We both knew this years ago. Your parents sent you to be 'fixed' when there was nothing to fix... and no need for such places that try to do it."

"But I was so convinced I was wrong. It was wrong. I believed it. I really thought I could change if I gave myself enough time."

"So that means that you weren't completely convinced by all this reconditioning."

"Well, no... but they told me I was possessed. And it would take some time before the demons left me."

"Oh for God's sake," Em said. "That amounts to emotional abuse."

Brandon put his hands over his face. "I'm so mixed up. What am I going to do?"

"Please, everyone, leave this to me," Sarah said as she stood up. "Come with me, dear. We need to have a little private talk." She pulled Brandon up, led him into the bedroom, and closed the door.

Mitch looked at Em.

"Don't look at me for answers. The woman continues to surprise me."

"Let's leave her to it and have some tea," Grady said, moving over to the tray and starting to pour tea into the remaining mugs.

"Still waters run deep," Mitch said.

"Hey," Em complained. "Old sayings are my province."

"Gotcha," Mitch said.

WHEN SARAH and Brandon finally returned to the living room, expectancy was tingling in the atmosphere.

"If it's all right with you, Mitch," Sarah stated, "Brandon is going to come home with me. He can stay in the spare bedroom, and he'll have time to do a lot of thinking without distractions."

135

"Sure," Mitch said, "whatever you want, Brandon."

"That's what I'd like. Sarah's been so good to me. I'm beginning to see things more clearly. I need some time alone, and Sarah and I think I might need to talk some more."

"Okay, then," Mitch replied. "It's settled. But we'll have to get you some new clothes. You come on over tomorrow, and we'll go shopping."

"Yes," Sarah added, "you can come over on the Path train with me."

It looked like Brandon might tear up again as he turned to Mitch. "You're such a good man, Mitch. After the things I said.... And you too, Grady. Can you forgive me? And you, Ms. Em. If I ever get out of line again, you've got to slap some sense into me."

Em smiled and crossed over to Brandon. She started to give him a little punch in the stomach, but pulled her fist at the last minute. Brandon responded with a huge "oooof" sound. "You're okay in my book, now," Em said. "But I'll keep my slapping hand in shape, just in case."

Brandon actually smiled, and Sarah beamed at her wife with much pride. Grady came over too and shook Brandon's hand.

"No hard feelings," he said.

"Thanks."

"I'll meet you two at the Path exit on Ninth Street at eleven or so," Mitch said.

Then Sarah and Em left with Brandon in tow, and, with great relief, Mitch closed the door behind them.

Mitch heaved a great sigh and flopped himself down next to Grady on the sofa. He let his spinning head fall onto the back of the sofa, heard a ghostly whisper, "Danger... hair oil...," and quickly lifted his head once again. He could feel Grady's body heat, and his pulse quickened. To avoid pulling the other man into his arms, he shifted so his back was against the arm, rather than the back of the sofa. Grady promptly took his usual position, leaning against the arm opposite. Mitch was comforted by the thought that they each had their assigned spot, his facing the kitchen and Grady facing the door. He liked the idea of each claiming his own spot now, without even thinking. This action screamed "family" to him.

"Families," Grady said, almost as if he'd heard Mitch's thoughts. "They are truly something else."

"Mine sure is."

"But from the way you talk about your family and your childhood, you always sound like it was a happy one."

"Oh, it was. I'm talking about Brandon's side of the family. They were always a little weird, but then they moved away, joined a cult, and became religious nuts."

"So, your two families were friends?"

"Friendly," Mitch replied. "Brandon's mother and my aunt Sue were sisters. My aunt Sue was the one who actually raised me. My parents are ardent archeologists and always seemed to be away on a 'dig,' as they called it. As a matter of fact, they still are. Then, if it was during the school year, my aunt would come down from her home in Calistoga—the home of the famous Calistoga water, you know—and take care of me. If it was the summer, I'd go to her place. Some summers, Brandon came with me. It was such fun. We'd go down to the 'crick' and float around on a raft we'd built."

Grady chuckled, a wonderful throaty sound that made Mitch tingle all over.

"No, my aunt was a truly wonderful woman. She told me many times that the most important human trait was what she called 'kindness of heart.' She always said it can't be taught—either a person has it or they don't… and, in her opinion, not many people had it."

"She sounds fantastic."

"She was. She took care of a neighbor woman who had nobody and was wheelchair-bound, so she could stay in the farmhouse she'd lived in for forty years. She raised two baby doves that had fallen out of their nest, and got teary-eyed when they were old enough to be on their own. She'd named them Spike and Rocky. She had quite a sense of humor. Everyone used the kitchen door as an entrance, but once in a while she'd hear a yowling at the front door, and would open it to find one of the cats had brought her a gift… a dead bird. She would pet the cat and thank it, and then go and bury the bird in a little bird cemetery she'd created with flowers and pretty rocks. She always said it was the cats' nature, and she couldn't blame them, no matter what she, herself, felt."

"Do you realize, Mitch, that you're exactly the same? 'Kindness of heart'—what a perfect phrase. She took care of birds, and you took care of me."

"Grady," he admonished. "That's hardly the same thing."

"It's the same impulse."

Mitch had no answer.

"It's a very," Grady went on, "very… loveable trait."

Mitch had to hold back a little gasp of surprise. Could this mean…?

He chanced a quick glance at Grady and saw intense blue eyes shining with… something. Did he dare to believe that Grady felt about him as he'd come to feel about Grady? Wishful thinking? But now, looking back, hadn't Grady given signs now and then? Perhaps he'd misinterpreted them, doubting his own instincts. He looked away in confusion.

"What about your family?" he asked quickly. "We've never really talked about them much. Except that you and Hank grew up together."

"Most of my lamentable background you already know. What I haven't mentioned yet is Hank's inheritance. That's how the condo came about. His mother was estranged from her father, his grandfather, over marrying below her station. He cut her off and wouldn't speak to her. But he left everything to Hank, the grandson he never even saw. And it was a lot."

"Wow."

"I never wanted the condo. He wanted me to do nothing but go to auditions and take classes, but I wanted to make my own way. I agreed to the condo because he said he wanted to enjoy the luxuries the money gave him. But I insisted that I pay my way. Not rent, that would have been sheer stubbornness, but I pitched in on groceries, et cetera, and I always had a job, admittedly a low-paying temp job, but I had to be as independent as I could. I wasn't brought up to be a sloth. I would have gone nuts."

"That's admirable," Mitch said.

"Not really."

"Oh, yes. I think a lot of people, probably most people, especially actors, would have jumped at the chance to do nothing but go to auditions. I have run across a few actors in my day."

"Well, this actor wasn't about to coast along on someone else's money."

"Wasn't that a difficult situation?"

"Yeah, sometimes I felt quite... I don't know... uneasy, put off, that things were so unequal. But he always said if the situation were reversed, I'd do the same thing. And, of course, even though I probably wouldn't have chosen such opulence, I certainly would have wanted him to share my good luck."

Mitch felt the tips of Grady's sock-clad foot, the one on the floor, brush against his own, and then give it a little nudge. As if it had a will of its own, his toes pushed back. Soon their toes began tangling and brushing against each other. It felt so good, both the friction and the contact itself. Mitch closed his eyes and let himself go with the feelings... until he felt himself begin to get aroused. No! This wouldn't do at all.

"Let... let's have another look at the costume sketches they sent you," he said, pulling his foot back. He looked up to find Grady staring at him intently.

"Sure," Grady replied after a moment, and he got up to retrieve the sketches. He returned with the envelope and sat down beside Mitch, who'd sat up and put both feet on the floor. Grady handed Mitch the envelope, then sat next to him as he opened it. There were two sketches—one profile and one full figure—of a male in a baby-blue-and-white-striped suit, with a little blue tie and a straw boater with a blue band. He had blue spats on his feet. Mitch had to smile.

"You're going to look so cute."

"I am not cute. I'm never cute," Grady said. "I keep telling you."

"Yes, you are. You can't help it. You just are."

Grady huffed in exasperation and gave Mitch a sharp nudge with his shoulder.

"I'm sorry, Grady, but you look so cute when you get mad at me for saying you look cute."

"You're just too much," Grady said, and he took Mitch by the shoulders and gave him a good shaking. The sketches slipped to the floor. Time seemed to morph into freeze-frame as Grady stopped shaking Mitch but left his hands on Mitch's shoulders. They exchanged a long look deep into each other's eyes. Mitch began to understand what the phrase drowning in someone's eyes really meant. He certainly felt like he just might be drowning in lustrous pools of blue.

Mitch got up suddenly and reached down to retrieve the sketches. "Good thing I didn't wreck these," he said, slipping the sheets back into the envelope.

"Right," Grady replied as he took the envelope from Mitch and put it back on the table. "Well, after all the drama tonight, I'm sort of shot," he said. "I think I'll turn in."

Mitch thought he heard a tone of resignation in Grady's voice, but perhaps it was just fatigue.

As Mitch watched Grady trudge down the hall to his room, he felt a sad sort of aching fill him. What a mess. What was he going to do?

And with that thought heavy on his mind, Mitch trudged off to his own room.

THE MORNING had started out rather gloomy, with an overcast sky of an unappealing gray. But by the time Mitch and Grady were ready to leave to meet Brandon and Sarah at the Path train, the sun had sent the clouds to wherever the clouds go when the sun decides it's time to take over the sky. Both wore Levi's, Mitch with a red T-shirt and Grady in a blue polo. They stopped at the Gourmet Garage on Seventh Avenue, which had an organic section, and each selected a beautiful Honeycrisp apple to take along. Mitch had only recently discovered that this store, in addition to its so-called "conventional" produce, had a huge section of organic and locally produced items. He'd been a devotee ever since.

As he bit into his apple and got the first crisp taste of its sweetness, he told Grady, "The first time I tried one of these, I thought to myself, 'This is how apples used to taste.'"

"I'm so glad you showed me this place. I think we get used to the beautiful, but relatively tasteless, fruit and vegetables the big chain stores give us. I noticed that the first time I had some homegrown tomatoes. What a difference. And now this place."

They continued to munch contentedly on their apples as they walked along the tree-shaded Charles Street to Sixth Avenue and saw Brandon and Sarah at the entrance to the Path train.

"Can't miss those two," Grady said, smiling.

"Not with Sarah being the only woman in sight with a hat, and Brandon in that horrible suit."

"I've got to hurry," Sarah said, after giving Mitch and Grady each a warm hug. "Emma and I are going to the Natural History Museum." She rushed off as the three men started up the sidewalk.

"Are we going to Bloomingdale's?" Brandon asked. Sometimes they were able to walk abreast, but more often it was single file, as the rush of people coming the other way, much like an ocean steamer, seemed determined not to alter their course one bit.

"Bloomingdale's?" Mitch replied. "You wouldn't catch me dead there."

"You don't like it either?" Grady asked.

"Nope. Way too snooty for me. The last time I walked through there, out of curiosity, I saw a rather plain Calvin Klein Sweater. I looked at the price and nearly fell over. It was $300. And this was years ago."

"I wouldn't buy a $300 sweater if Calvin Klein knitted it himself!" Grady added.

This got a huge chuckle from Brandon, who'd taken his suit jacket off and had it slung over his shoulder. Mitch thought he looked infinitely better.

"Barneys?" he asked

"No way," Mitch said. "I have a personal bone to pick with Barneys."

"Why? What's that about?" Brandon said.

"They used to have a great store down in the Village, as well as the one uptown. Ironically, the one in the Village is where Loehmann's—you know, their bags say, 'I just got a bargain'—is now. But Barneys closed the Village location and stuck with the Upper East Side… where all the well-to-do live. I felt betrayed."

Grady chuckled and gave Mitch a smack on the arm. Mitch was delighted.

141

"How about Banana Republic?" Brandon said. With the slight wind blowing through his hair, now free of gel, and being so much more relaxed, he looked much as Mitch remembered him. Just a nice-looking regular guy. He seemed so comfortable being with Mitch and Grady, as if they'd been on many shopping trips before.

"Banana Republic, the Gap, and Old Navy are all owned by the same people," Mitch told him. "Banana Republic is supposedly top tier of the three, followed by the Gap and then comes Old Navy. But I like the stuff at Old Navy so much better."

"And it's so much cheaper," Grady added. "That's where this shirt came from." He pulled at the blue polo shirt. "It was on sale for twelve dollars. How could I resist?"

"Do you suppose your shirt and mine are cousins?" Mitch said. "That's where all my T-shirts come from."

"How about Macy's?" Brandon was still weighing his options.

"Too old fuddy-duddy for me," Mitch said.

"Too what?" Brandon asked as he turned around and started walking backward, facing Mitch and Grady.

"Too conservative," Grady supplied. "Too much for the older crowd."

By grabbing Brandon and pulling him aside, they barely avoided a catastrophe as the trio, with Brandon walking backward, was on a collision course with a man pushing a market basket grossly overloaded with everything from an old withered broom to a huge stuffed bear. The wheels squeaked unpleasantly as he passed them, muttering.

"There's two of my favorite places," Mitch said as they approached Old Navy. "Just a block away. The Container Store on our left and Bed Bath & Beyond on our right. I could get lost in either one... like I was in a museum."

"One time I got so involved at Bed Bath & Beyond, I missed an audition," Grady said.

"Wow."

"I had to sneak in there," he added. "Hank thought the place was too low-class, and I couldn't stand his ranting about it every time I wanted to walk through."

"And we all know what impeccable taste old Hank has," Mitch said, almost snarling.

Grady didn't say anything, but the look he gave Mitch said a lot.

Mitch pulled one of the gray double doors open, and they trooped through them and the second set of doors several feet farther on. As they walked into the welcome coolness of the store, they were greeted by a group of people—men, women, children of all races—and a dog, frozen in a pleasing tableau. Of course, they were all display figures dressed in Old Navy clothes. Except for the dog; he was just wearing his own plaster fur.

The first floor being devoted to women's apparel, clothing on the left and little islands of jewelry and dark glasses, purses, and such on the right, Mitch led them toward the back of the store, where the escalator to the lower level, the men's section, was located. As the escalator carried them downward and the men's section appeared more and more in view, Mitch got the satisfied feeling he always felt at this point. He really, really liked this store. Everything was so sporty and youthful. He never came down this way without buying at least something. To him it was impossible.

Also, the customers reflected the figures at the door, and people of every stripe wandered here and there. As they neared the bottom of the escalator, Mitch quickly glanced left to a display that usually held an array of either T-shirts or polo shirts. That day it was striped polo shirts. On sale, they were two for fifteen dollars. Mitch selected one in warm colors and one in cool colors.

"How about these?" he asked Brandon.

"Whatever you think, Mitch. I've been out of things for too long."

"Grady?" Mitch asked.

"I think they'd be perfect for Brandon. Bring out his natural beauty." He clapped Brandon on the shoulder playfully.

"Right," Brandon replied.

"No, seriously, I think you'd look really good in them."

Brandon smiled. "Then I think you should get a few too."

Mitch was delighted that they seemed comfortable enough to tease each other. Then Mitch steered them to the left, where the entire wall was taken up with shelves of T-shirts in every color known to man. It looked like the proverbial rainbow.

"Here we go. Turquoise, salmon, yellow, green, blue, and red. The whole spectrum."

"Jeez, Mitch," Brandon said, "that's way too many."

"Nonsense. We have to get you off to a good start. Now," he added, turning back to the left and toward the back of the store, where there were racks upon racks of shirts. He pulled a nice plaid in blues, with cowboy snaps instead of buttons, off a crowded rack. "How about this one?"

"Okay," Brandon said, sounding pleasantly overwhelmed.

Grady stepped forward and took the shirt out of Mitch's hands. "This would look terrific on you, Mitch," he said. He held the shirt up to Mitch, pinning it against his chest, with his thumbs where Mitch's deltoids and his pectoral joined on each side.

"Aren't I right, Brandon?" Grady asked while continuing to hold the shirt against Mitch.

"Yeah, only I'd better get another color or we'll look like the Bobbsey twins."

"Mitch?"

Mitch could only feel the warm pressure of Grady's thumbs on his shoulders and was only able to nod agreement. Grady smiled and drew another shirt off the rack in shades of green for Brandon.

"Socks," Mitch was finally able to mutter.

"What?" Brandon said.

"Socks and underwear. In the back." He moved as though through glue toward the back of the store.

Halfway there, Grady said, "Do they have a men's room here?"

"I suppose so," Mitch mumbled. "I've never had to ask."

"You two go ahead. I'll catch up with you."

As Grady took off, Mitch led Brandon, who had both arms draped with clothes, toward the back of the store. He stopped to look at a couple of tables of workout clothes, absently picked up a slinky black top, and then, finally gathering up his wayward wits, he moved on.

"You really like him, don't you?" Brandon said.

144

"Hmmm?"

"I said, Grady, you really like him, don't you?"

As if they were once again teenage confidants, Mitch said, "Ah, Brandon, what am I going to do? I didn't mean for this to happen. It just… just… sort of snuck up on me."

"But I can tell Grady's a great guy. Why shouldn't you fall for him?"

Mitch pulled Brandon into the workout clothes section, which was empty at the moment.

"He's just been through a terrible breakup. I don't think he's in any way up for a new romance."

"I think you're dead wrong."

"What?"

"Sarah and I have been discussing it. Apparently, she's convinced, and so is Em. In fact, Em is about to slap you silly if you don't say something. And haven't you noticed the way he looks at you? Like you're candy and cake all rolled into one. He dotes on you, my friend."

"No… I…."

"I even got it when I first saw you two in your apartment, you know, when I was still evil Brandon."

"Let's not even go there—let's figure that era was just a bad dream. No, Bran, what I worry about is that he'll think I'm after some kind of payback for letting him stay with me."

"Mitch, he's been with you long enough to know that's simply not your style, that you would never take advantage of anybody."

"But what if you're wrong?"

Just then two rather loud types came into the sports section, and Mitch quickly drew Brandon over near the socks/underwear part of the store.

"It would kill me," Mitch continued, "if I thought for even one second that Grady suspected me of that. I knew from the moment I met him that he was gorgeous. But I didn't respond. As you might remember, I've been sort of emotionally dead for a long time. My feelings snuck up on me. He's such a good guy, so much fun, so smart, so talented…."

145

"So loveable?"

Mitch thought what a strange conversation this was to be having surrounded by displays of underwear, both briefs and boxers, plain and patterned.

"Yeah," he said softly, "so damned loveable."

"Here he comes now. Mitch, for God's sake, don't blow this."

Grady walked jauntily toward them carrying a large blue canvas bag with "Old Navy" stenciled on the side.

"What's that for?" Mitch asked as he approached.

"For recycling, naturally. When we check out, we won't have to use any plastic bags."

"See, Mitch?" Brandon said pointedly. "Grady thinks of everything."

"Mmm," Mitch replied, grabbing a couple packages of socks. "You can pick out your own underwear. Still a briefs man, I suppose?"

"At least that never changed," Brandon replied, growing a bit red in the face as he snatched up a couple of packages.

Smiling broadly, Grady asked, "Now what?"

"Now we go back upstairs," Mitch said, leading them to the up silver-treaded escalator, which was only a few feet away.

As they stood in the checkout line, which snaked back and forth near the cash registers, Mitch said, "We'll have to go to a Levi's store for some jeans. No designer jeans for us, and we can get you some New Balance shoes on the Internet."

They watched the little on and off green lights until one signaled that it was their turn. As the cashier rang up the mound of clothes, Grady proudly plopped each purchase into the canvas bag. When they were done, it looked like a big blue stuffed sausage.

As Mitch and Grady started to argue over who was going to carry it, Brandon stepped in and snatched the handles.

"This was all for me, so it's only fair that I carry it." And he marched toward the door.

"I think Brandon is getting his confidence back," Grady said.

Mitch chuckled. "It's like I've got my old friend back."

And they followed Mitch's "old friend" out of the store.

When they finally got back to Mitch's apartment, Brandon headed for Grady's room to try on his new clothes in front of the full-length mirror there, as Mitch and Grady each went his own way.

When Mitch finally went into his own room, he found a beautiful peach-colored T-shirt on his bed. He crossed over, picked it up, and turned around to find a smiling Grady leaning against the doorway.

"You didn't."

"I did."

"How? When?"

"I didn't have to go to the men's room. I just looped back, got it, and then went upstairs and paid for it."

"But I didn't see...."

"That's the main reason I bought the big canvas bag. It was in there."

"You're quite a sneak."

"Yeah, aren't I?"

Mitch crossed to his dresser, opened a door, and pulled out an identical T-shirt, only in a rich purple. He held it up.

"You didn't."

"I did." Mitch tossed the T-shirt to Grady, who caught it easily.

"How?"

"I slipped it in and distracted you when the cashier rang it up. Luckily, Brandon was already packing things double-time."

"Sneaky."

"Yeah, aren't I?"

They both broke up and crossed to each other, clinging as they found themselves in a laughing fit. Mitch thought his heart would explode

But it didn't.

Chapter Eight

MITCH HEARD a strange knocking sound coming from the door to his apartment.

Woodpecker?

Then the bell gave several frantic rings, like its life was in danger and it was calling for help. But Grady had his key, and Em had her special ring, so it couldn't be either of them. He strode hastily to the door and swung it open to find Grady peeking through a huge bouquet of flowers, with a bottle of wine in the other hand.

"Quick," Grady gasped, rushing by, "the bottle is slipping out of my hand!" He ran to the sofa and let the bottle fall onto the cushions. Then he adjusted the flowers and turned to Mitch with a huge grin on his face.

"What's all this?" Mitch said, puzzled.

"Well, you said that you'd never received flowers and wine, and I thought that was a shame and that I should do something about it."

"But... I...."

"Here," Grady said, rushing forward and shoving the flowers into Mitch's hands. "Roses," he added.

The incredibly heady perfume of roses filled Mitch's senses. He inhaled deeply until he almost felt dizzy. Then he, in turn, peeked through the roses... at least two dozen... and returned Grady's grin.

"Jeez, Grady, you're too much. I... I've never had anyone bring me flowers or wine before. I don't know what to say. Thanks doesn't seem enough."

"The look on your face is thanks enough."

They stood like that, grinning at each other with happy smiles.

"I'd better put these in water," Mitch finally muttered, and he turned away, heading for the kitchen. He pulled a cut glass Baccarat vase from a high shelf in a cupboard and filled it with water. As he ripped the paper from the bouquet, Grady joined him, pulled open a drawer, and withdrew a pair of scissors.

"Here," he said.

"What's that for?"

"You're supposed to cut the stem at a forty-five degree angle under lukewarm running water."

"How do you know that?"

"Sarah told me when I asked her what kind of flowers I should get. She said it keeps them from wilting too fast. And you're supposed to put a shot or two of lemon/lime soda in the vase too."

"We don't have any kind of soda."

"I don't think it matters that much. We can get some for next time."

"Next time. You mean you plan on doing this again?"

"I certainly do."

Mitch just shook his head, but a warm wave slowly crept up his body. A feeling, he thought, much like the gradual reverse pleasure of slipping into warm bathwater.

"Oh," Grady said, "and no aspirin. Sarah said that's a fallacy. Aspirin does absolutely nothing to preserve the flowers."

"You're just a fount of knowledge. I'm impressed."

"Not me. Thank Sarah, the gardener."

After he finished cutting the flowers and placing them in the vase, Mitch pulled them up to his face and inhaled again.

"Beautiful," he said.

Grady leaned forward to get a whiff of the roses himself, and they bumped heads.

"Ow," they both said at once and then began chuckling.

Mitch stopped suddenly and looked straight into Grady's eyes.

"You're such a good guy," he said softly.

"No...."

"Who else would remember a casual remark and then do something like this?"

"Someone who appreciates the fact that you probably saved his sanity."

Now Mitch was embarrassed; he hurried back into the living room and placed the vase on the side of his desk.

"Where I can look at them all the time." He turned to Grady and knew the look in his own eyes betrayed way too much. Grady stepped toward him just as the doorbell rang, followed by the ever-present two knocks.

"Em," they both said at once, "always Em!"

But it was Sarah who entered, carrying a small bottle of lemon/lime soda.

"I thought you probably wouldn't have this on hand," she said. She crossed to Mitch's desk, where the flowers gloried in their crystal vase.

"Oh, Salutes," she said, "such a lovely strain. A perfect choice." She poured a bit of soda into the vase. "Salutes are in the class called Burgundy Roses, and you know what that means."

"No," said Grady.

"No," said Mitch a second later.

"Well, rose lore would have it that Burgundy Roses reveal unconscious beauty and are perfect for the shy lover."

Mitch felt his face flush with an unaccustomed blush. He turned to Grady and realized they'd both turned pretty much the color of the roses.

Sarah giggled, a rather strange little sound for such a tall woman. "Em," she called out, "it's your turn."

And on cue, Emma stepped through the partially open door, carrying a white box with a big red bow stuck on the top.

"Grady couldn't manage everything," she explained. She walked over to Grady and handed him the box.

"More?" Mitch said, bewildered. Grady backed him up a few steps until Mitch felt the back of his legs hit the sofa. He sat. Grady placed the box in his lap and knelt on the floor in front of him.

"Yes, more," Grady said.

Emma and Sarah crowded closer.

Mitch slowly pulled the top off the box, and out tumbled a wiggling brown heap of puppy.

"It's a dachshund," the ladies said together.

The puppy turned big soft brown eyes on Mitch and licked his hand. Mitch was a goner. He loved this puppy.

Just like he loved… might as well admit it.

"Look." Grady broke into his wayward thoughts. "He has about an inch of black hairs on the end of his tail."

Sarah said, "Grady told us that most of the litter was already spoken for. Most people hoped for a show dog and didn't want any, what they called, blemishes."

"Blemish, indeed," Em put in. "I think it only makes him cuter. It makes him special."

"Right," Grady added, "and remember, you told me the dog you had had no hair on the end of his tail because it was worn off from hitting the floor when he wagged it so much. I thought maybe that was a portent."

"I'm not sure I believe in portents," Mitch said.

"Well, if it's a coincidence," Em put in, "it must be one in ten billion."

"Exactly," Sarah agreed.

"Okay, you guys win. It was a portent." The puppy now seemed perfectly content to lie still in Mitch's lap while Mitch petted him and ran his fingers along his long soft ears.

"I thought," Grady said as he sat on the floor at Mitch's feet, the only place left, since Em and Sarah in their excitement had taken their places on either side, crowding him, "you might want to call him Pretzel Two."

"No," Mitch answered slowly, "I've read it's not a good idea to name a second pet after a deceased first one."

"Well, you've got to call him something," Em said, sneaking a quick pat on the puppy's head.

Mitch gazed up at the patterns of the beams on the ceiling as he gave this important matter considerable thought. The others waited in anticipation.

"I think," Mitch said finally, "I'm going to call him Puppy."

"Puppy?" Grady said.

"I always call dogs puppy. Here, Puppy. Cute Puppy. Stop it, Puppy. So I might just as well call him Puppy. I always call cats Kitty."

"You've never called Tweet 'Birdy.'"

"Tweet already had a name."

"Okay, Puppy it is," Grady said as he stood up. "Now if one of you… not Puppy… will hand me the champagne that someone must be sitting on, I'll get glasses and propose a toast."

"Wise guy," Em said. "It slipped back behind the cushion." She reached behind her and pulled out the bottle.

"You'd better be careful when you open it," Sarah said. "With all the jostling around, it just might explode."

"I will," Grady said, leaving the room.

They heard the musical clinking of stemware hitting each other, and then a loud bang, as the cork hit the ceiling, and then a foaming noise and splashes on the floor.

"Dammit!" Grady muttered.

The three of them started to laugh.

"If I hear the slightest chuckle," Grady said, obviously through gritted teeth, "I swear I'll pour what's left down the sink."

Three hands quickly covered three mouths, and three bodies shook so much that it woke the puppy up, and he began to struggle from one lap to the other. When Grady finally returned to the room, he found three frozen figures, Em with her hands over her ears, Mitch with his hands over his eyes, and Sarah with her hands over her mouth.

"Very funny," he said. "Mocking a poor, drenched, almost-drowned being in his extreme distress. One with soaked Levi's and wet feet."

This broke the tableau up, and all four of them started laughing as Grady put the tray with four half-filled champagne flutes on the coffee table. He'd kicked off his shoes, and was, indeed, soaking wet and dripping from the knees down.

Each of them picked up a champagne flute.

"What shall we toast?" Em asked.

"Something profound," Sarah added.

"Here's to fond friends," Mitch finally said.

"And to new beginnings," Grady added.

They drank.

"That was the best half glass of champagne I ever had," Em quipped as she stood up.

"I think we'd better be going," Sarah said, joining her. "You boys have to settle the puppy and make him feel at home."

Arm in arm, they headed toward the door. Over her shoulder Em gave Mitch a "significant" look.

IN THE days following, their established routine continued. Grady would go to work, and Mitch would then type away on his novel, but always with the thought of Grady and when he would come through the door fleeting through his head like a frightened rabbit running for its life from a fox. If he thought about Grady too much, he would forget about his work and dream impossible dreams. Dreams of them being together—not just now, but forever. In a state of suspended bliss, he envisioned them living much as they did at present, but not in separate bedrooms. No, they would be a real couple; they might even decide to mimic Em and Sarah and run to Massachusetts and get married. Then Puppy would have two parents, instead of just one. Of course the union wouldn't be legal in New York, but in their minds they would be formally united as a couple. And, who knew, someday perhaps New York would follow its more enlightened neighbor.

He would suddenly come out of his trance and realize none of it was true and plunge into reality, much like that first shocking moment diving into an early fall ocean. It would take him some time to return to his work. So he tried to keep his thoughts swift and short-lived.

When Grady came through the door, now working only half days and spending the rest of his time studying lines and lyrics, a tide of warmth flooded Mitch. He would then relax, as if somehow an impending disaster had once again been averted. They would talk comfortably about the routine of their day, and then Em and Sarah would arrive for that day's rehearsal.

Grady would go through his lines while Mitch or Em or Sarah read the other parts. Then Grady and Sarah would go through his music, and Mitch and Em would provide the enthusiastic audience. When Grady was satisfied that they'd done as much as possible during the allotted time, they would crowd into Mitch's kitchen and collaborate on dinner, much the way they collaborated on *Carousel*. They would chat and laugh as they ate, very comfortable with each other.

However, Mitch's anxiety grew with every passing day. He dreaded Grady's departure but had to hide his feelings so Grady would be able to enjoy this theater venture to its utmost without any worries about Mitch. By Saturday, with the last four performances of *Othello* beginning next week, he found it difficult to think about anything else. His writing suffered, and, more often than not, many pages ended up being deleted when he read them over and found them wanting.

Mitch was trying to get his thoughts in order when he heard Grady's key in the door. When Grady came through the doorway, Mitch didn't have to force the smile that came to his face—it was there the minute he saw Grady's familiar form come in and shut the door.

"Hi," Grady said, his own smile reflecting Mitch's. "How's it going?"

"As well as it can be expected at this point," Mitch answered, not wanting to outright lie to Grady. "We'd better get ready—Em and Sarah are due any minute."

Grady took off for his room, and Mitch straightened up his desk, then got the keyboard ready on its stand. When Grady returned in Levi's and a tight black T-shirt, Mitch could only think that no matter how handsome Grady looked in a suit, he was absolutely devastating in casual clothes. The doorbell rang, and the ladies were there.

After greetings and hugs all around, they got down to work. They began with the music to vary the rehearsal a bit but had only gotten a few bars into the song when the phone rang. Mitch hurried to answer and motioned for the others to go on.

"It's Brandon," he said in a puzzled tone. Brandon had pretty much recovered from his near breakdown, thanks to Sarah's help and advice. She'd confided her history to Brandon, and they had formed a sort of bond of kindred souls who had fought similar demons.

"What?" Mitch shouted. The tone of his voice brought the others to an abrupt silence. "And he what?"

After listening intently, Mitch gave the other three a very grim look.

"Okay. Just hold on. We'll be right there."

"Right where?" Em asked.

"I think we'd all better sit down for just a second," Mitch said.

"That sounds ominous," Sarah said.

After they were all seated, Mitch reluctantly began his story.

"Apparently, Sarah, your son stopped by your house and found Brandon there. When he asked who the devil Brandon was, Brandon told him how kind you'd been to him, how you'd helped him own his gayness, and that he was so happy for you and Em."

"Oh, no," Sarah whispered.

"And your son went berserk and started hollering that his mother was no lesbo and that this bastard—that being Brandon—better get out of his house. Brandon tried to reason with him, but it was no use."

"Oh, my God," Em said, and she took a weeping Sarah into her arms.

"Brandon wasn't about to leave, so he ran into the bathroom and locked the door. He had his new cell phone latched onto his hip, and he called us. Your son is now pounding on the door and threatening death."

"Now what?" Grady asked.

"I told him we'd be right there and to hang on as best he could."

"I can't. I can't," Sarah pleaded.

Em sat back and took both Sarah's hands in her own. "Sarah, dear, you have to confront him. There's no other way."

"But, Em…."

"Unless you want an annulment," she said, apparently hoping humor might lighten this sodden moment.

Sarah just looked at Em with a conflicted expression.

155

"We'll be right there for you too," Grady said. "You can count on that."

Mitch stood and very seriously stated, "You're my little family and I won't let anyone hurt any of you. We'll get through this together. All right?"

Grady stood with a quick, grateful look at Mitch and then turned to Sarah. "Right," he added.

Em helped Sarah to her feet, and, supporting her, started toward the door.

"With an army like this, how can we not prevail?" Em said as they all hurried out of the apartment.

Mitch insisted on driving, and once he'd backed the Dodge out of the garage, Em helped Sarah into the backseat where she held her and tried to calm her down. Grady shut the garage door and jumped in the front seat with Mitch. The car door had barely slammed shut when Mitch took off like he was trying out for the Indianapolis 500.

Grady whispered so only Mitch could hear, "At least this will take Sarah's mind off her troubles. She'll be too busy fearing death."

Mitch had to smile in spite of the seriousness of their trip. He appreciated the mild humor, as it helped him relax. He had to grin, not only at Grady's little joke, but at the fact that he was driving as badly, or probably worse, than he'd chided Em for on their last trip to Hoboken. He chuckled.

"What's so funny up there?" Em asked.

"I was just thinking that your horrible driving must be contagious. Look how I'm going along, something like a meteor."

"Any slower and I'd have to take over," Em told him.

In the rearview mirror, Mitch notice that Sarah was smiling at Em. He was relieved that Em had managed to quiet her. It had been unnerving to watch the usually calm, competent Sarah fall apart. This was more like it.

They zoomed into the Holland Tunnel. There was a blur of bright lights and the rumbling of many cars, but he didn't even think once about the water above or the chance it might start pouring onto the roadway.

They exited the tunnel much as they'd entered it, like a shell from a cannon.

"Slow, slow," Grady whispered.

By then, Mitch saw the slower traffic ahead and had to stomp on the brakes.

"Move, move," Mitch said through gritted teeth. "Come on, you guys, stop trying to imitate turtles."

As the cars ahead moved, Mitch started to turn as they had on their first trip to Hoboken.

"No, no, no," Sarah exclaimed, "turn right. It's faster to go down Frank Sinatra Boulevard. There's no stoplights, so less traffic."

Mitch swung to the right, and soon they were on their way.

"Frank Sinatra Boulevard?" Grady snorted.

"He was a local boy," Sarah told them. "Our most famous alumnus."

"I never liked his voice," Grady said. "I like Tony Bennett much better."

With less traffic Mitch was able to take in his surroundings once again. To his right was a fantastic view of Manhattan; to him it was even better than the Brooklyn Heights Promenade, and he felt that was hard to beat. All along his left was the rocky side of a mountainous outcropping. Finding the right side more interesting, he noticed several joggers, a couple of bicyclists, some skateboarders, and several people sitting on benches enjoying the view. He caught the sparkles reflecting off the water like millions of little mirrors. The heady scent of the ocean permeated the car, replacing the automobile fumes that had taken over during the ride through the tunnel.

In the backseat, Sarah seemed a bit more like her old self, but she still clung to Em, who had continued speaking softly to her.

"I always favored Billy Eckstine," Em said.

"What?" Mitch answered.

"You were comparing Frank Sinatra to other singers."

"Yeah, quite a while ago."

"I'm giving you a D in 'pays attention.'"

"Oh, don't, Em," Grady said. "It'll destroy him."

"I won't dignify that remark with an answer," Mitch told them grandly. "Can't beat Perry Como," he added pointedly.

"How about Herb Jeffries?" Grady said.

"Who?" the other three chorused.

"Same era. You know, when the songs had real lyrics and melody lines."

"How about the ladies?" Mitch said. "From that same time."

"Doris Day," Sarah said quickly.

"A tie between Rosemary Clooney and Dinah Washington," Em said.

Grady smiled and added, "The one and only Peggy Lee."

They all looked at Mitch. He waited a bit to let them wonder.

"Kay Starr," he said finally. "'Wheel of Fortune.'"

So intent had they been on their musical tastes that they only now realized they were driving down Hudson Street toward Sarah's home. Mitch pulled into the parking space behind the house and they hurried up the sidewalk and crossed the garden, stepping lightly on the ladybug-shaped stepping-stones. The front door was open, and they could hear wild shouting from inside.

"Come out of there, you slimy son of a bitch. I'm going to beat your faggot head in."

"That's David, my son," Sarah whispered.

Em stepped forward into the living room, put her hands on her hips, and shouted, "Come here, you good-for-nothing. Come here and apologize to your mother!"

The shouting stopped, and a tall, chunky, dark-haired man came staggering into the room. His hair was wild, and his clothes looked like he'd recently rolled down a hill in them. His shirttail was out, and his tie was hanging loosely over his shoulder.

"Who the hell are you?" he yelled at Em.

"You just shut up," she told him.

Mitch and Grady had created a wall between him and Sarah to protect her as best they could from this barrage. But then her son caught sight of her, Sarah being so tall that even two sturdy guys like Mitch and Grady couldn't completely hide her.

"Mama," he said with an angry look, "is it true? What that idiot told me, is it true? You have… a… a… what… girlfriend?"

Mitch and Grady turned to look at the stricken Sarah, who stood absolutely still as if she'd turned into a statue.

Mitch watched as realization slowly came over David's face.

"It is true!" he yelled. "You're a damned lesbo! My mother is queer. How could you?"

Mitch and Grady stepped aside to give Sarah room as she took a step toward her son, holding her hands out.

"No," he hollered, stepping back, "don't come near me! Don't you touch me! My mother has a… a… girlfriend, she—"

"That would be me!" Em said as she strode right up to him.

A bewildered and distraught Brandon staggered into the room. He quickly took in the scene and froze a few paces beyond David.

"You're… you're what?" David exclaimed.

"The girlfriend," Em repeated, staring up at him as she might at a tall building. She was dwarfed by the man. "That's me. Or the wife, to be perfectly correct. I—"

"The what? The *wife*? Why, you abomination."

"Watch what you say," Brandon interjected quickly. "Don't make her angry, or you'll regret it deeply."

Mitch watched as the word that Brandon had used on meeting her seeped into Em's understanding. He figured he knew what was coming.

Sure enough, Em leaped up and slapped him soundly across the face. And then, to prove her point, she backhanded him on the way down.

"How dare you talk like that to your mother? Now you just watch it, or I may have to really hurt you."

When Mitch saw that David might not take Em's warning seriously, he came forward, followed by Grady, and they each took one of his arms as they forced him over to the sofa and unceremoniously sat him down. They squeezed him between them so he couldn't move. Now he was on a level lower than Em; that seemed to help her control herself, with great effort.

"Listen to me, David," she said in her no-nonsense teacher voice. "You don't know what heartache your mother has gone through. At least hear her story, and if you still feel the way you do now, just go away. No more hollering, in any case. It doesn't do any good. All right?"

Brandon slipped cautiously along and sat on the piano bench. Sarah still stood in the same place. During the melee, she'd gotten her bright little handkerchief out, and she was dabbing her eyes. Em went to her and put her arm around her.

"Your mother is a wonderful person. Kind and gentle, and if you don't want a rift that will cause you to lose her, you'd better stop being so judgmental and hear her story."

David seemed to deflate, and Mitch felt all the tension leave him.

"I really don't know if I can come to terms with this. I...."

"Just try," Em told him.

"If you desert her," Mitch told him, "we'll be more than happy to take your place. Right, Grady?"

"She's part of our family already."

"There you have it," Em said. "As you can see, your mother is very well loved. But she still needs her son, and that position, my boy, only you can fill. Now we'll all go in the kitchen and make some nice tea while you two have a serious talk. Call us when you're through."

Mitch turned David loose and stood up as Grady joined him. Together with Em and Brandon, they left the room and headed toward the kitchen. A few steps into the hallway, Mitch whispered to the others, "You go ahead. I'm going to stick around for a bit, just to make sure they get off to a fairly civilized start."

As the others continued on into the kitchen, where Mitch soon heard the clinking of cups and saucers, and then the running of water for tea, he crept a few steps back toward the living room. Hugging the textured wallpaper, he slowly crept forward as he certainly didn't want to disturb what must be a serious and very frightening conversation. When he stopped, Mitch found he could watch the proceedings in a mirror on the opposing wall. He couldn't help noticing that it was an old-fashioned mirror in the shape of a rather squashed bell curve, with a regular silver center panel with two pink sidepieces beveled in diamond shapes. It would look beautiful anywhere, particularly over his mantel. In it he now saw David sitting forward, his elbows on his knees and his head in his hands. Sarah sat absolutely still except for the tears that streamed down her cheeks. Mitch could barely keep himself from rushing into the room and taking the sweet and gentle Sarah in his arms, consoling her.

"Mama," David finally said, his voice hoarse with spent emotion, "please stop crying. I've never seen you cry. Not once."

Sarah didn't answer. She just kept dabbing at her eyes.

Mitch watched David sit back against the sofa cushions.

"Tell me this story of yours those people were talking about," he finally ground out after a long silence.

A long sigh shuddered out of Sarah, and slowly she began relating the tragedy that had overtaken her in high school.

Mitch was torn between leaving his hidden spot and staying in place. He didn't want to eavesdrop, but he had a feeling that staying where he was and sending supportive thoughts to Sarah would somehow help her. He was in no way metaphysical in his convictions, but leaving felt to him like he was deserting her. While he was ruminating, Sarah must have finished her story, as Mitch became aware of the awful silence surrounding the two on the sofa.

"But what about Dad?" David finally asked.

"Oh... oh, David, I did love your father. He... he was a kind, wonderful man. I just wasn't... in love... with him. And... and sadly, there is a big difference."

"But you seemed happy. Weren't you happy?"

"Of course I was happy. As happy as I could be."

"Wasn't that enough?"

"I always thought so."

"What changed?"

"When your father died, I became so lonely. So lonely. And my... my thoughts kept coming back to those earlier years."

"But... but you'd changed. How could you go back?"

"Oh, David, my dear, a person can't really... 'change'... as you say. Perhaps in some situations they can... how shall I put it... they can channel their feelings."

"But...."

"Let me ask you something, David: Could you just change your orientation?"

"Of course not."

"Well, it's the same for me and for plenty of others."

"Way to go, Sarah," Mitch whispered to himself. She was handling this very, very well.

"I thought you went on that cruise to… to regroup."

"I did. It was all… all… ladies, you know. I just meant to observe."

"And…."

"And then Emma happened."

Mitch watched Sarah's smile appear for the first time that afternoon.

"And that's who… your… your girlfriend?" David asked, a touch of rancor slipping back into his voice. "The little one who goes around slapping people?" His hand crept up to the red mark on his cheek. "Hard," he added.

Sarah sat up straighter. "Don't you say a word against Emma. I won't hear of it. She's been so very good to me. As have her friends. I've seldom felt so accepted."

Mitch watched David slump down again. His image in the beveled part of the mirror now was a mass of diffracted pieces.

"And… and…" His voice cracked. "I suppose you really didn't want me… you know, to complicate things. You…."

"David, no," Sarah exclaimed. "You are my darling son. Of course I wanted you. I treasure you."

"Oh."

"Is that what you thought?"

"Yes. I think that's why I lost it. The first thing that came to mind was that you probably never wanted me. That you never were happy with Dad or me."

Mitch felt himself choking up as Sarah took her son in her arms.

"You must know one thing: you are precious to me. I love you. Even if you leave me, I'll still love you. You're my son."

"I won't ever leave you."

Mitch could barely hear the words, they were spoken so softly.

"We'll talk some more tonight," Sarah said, rising. "Let me tell my friends to go on home. I don't want them out there in the kitchen thinking the worst."

Mitch crept backward hurriedly to the kitchen, grabbed up the first teacup he could see, and took his place with the others.

"We've talked," Sarah said as she joined them. "I think… I think everything will work out in time. David's going to stay here with me for a while so we can hash this out. Oh, don't worry, I'll still make time to go over the music and spend time with all of you."

"Should I leave?" Brandon asked, his voice shaking just a bit.

"Of course not. What was formerly the guest room is now your room for as long as you want it. In fact, I think your being here will help my situation a great deal."

"That's a relief," Brandon said candidly.

Em crossed to Sarah and took her by both hands. "I'm so proud of you, Sarah. You handled this perfectly. You know, I'll always be there for you."

"And me too," Grady added.

"And me," Mitch said.

"Ditto," said Brandon.

Sarah smiled warmly.

With great relief, the others left, Em casting a "determined" glance at David as she passed him.

He frowned.

"Em," Mitch warned.

"Never mind. I take care of my own!"

The ride back was uneventful.

Mitch sent his thanks right through the top of the car and heavenward.

Chapter Nine

THE FINELY tuned routine they'd all established before the "Hoboken Incident," as they came to call it, continued with minor adjustments. Sarah spent mornings at her home, talking at length with both Brandon and her son, David. She seemed much relieved that the crisis had crept quietly away, and the three of them were growing more and more comfortable in each other's presence. Em spent her mornings with her custodial duties and had tea with Mitch often. One morning she'd actually brought crumpets to go with the tea.

"How very English of you," Mitch had quipped.

"I always wondered what they were like," Em said. "And when I saw these in the store, I couldn't resist."

"Mmm," Mitch murmured, enjoying the buttery crumpet.

"They're quite tasty," Em said. "Kind of like muffins of the English persuasion, only a bit blander, and not so crunchy. They're better for you too. No fat."

"Mmm," Mitch repeated as he slathered the lemon curd, which Em had also supplied, on the last bit of crumpet and stuffed it into his mouth. When he finally could speak, he first emitted a very contented sigh.

"I always thought the term 'lemon curd' sounded perfectly nauseating, but it's just like the filling in a lemon meringue pie. And I dearly love lemon meringue pie."

"Not more than chocolate!"

"Well, no. Chocolate reigns supreme."

"Good. I'd hate to think of you being such a traitor."

"You realize we all have our own little morning duties these days. I write, Grady goes to work part time, Sarah counsels, and you do your landlady thing and bring me goodies. Then we all meet for our musical afternoon."

"You know," Em said, "I miss Sarah now that she has to spend more time in Hoboken. But I'm so glad that things are working out with David. She's so much happier not having to hide anything from him. She feels they've grown closer than ever, and, of course, that makes me very happy."

"It won't be forever, Em, just until they both get accustomed to the new people they've become."

"Oh, I know. I feel sort of selfish to want so much of her time, but I can't help it."

"Of course you can't. It's human nature to want to be near the person you care most about."

"I wouldn't say anything so mushy to anybody but you, dear," Em said softly. "But she becomes more precious to me every day. She's such a good soul."

"As are you, Em. I think you deserve each other."

"Do you?" Mitch saw the tears forming in her eyes, and he knew she'd be embarrassed to have him see her as anything but the image of strength. He needed to say something.

"Yes, you deserve each other. Sugar and spice. Chili powder, actually."

"Little wretch," Em said, smiling. She stood up and headed for the door. "See you later," she threw over her shoulder, as she quickly left, like the whirlwind she always mimicked.

Mitch took their dishes and the leftover crumpets and lemon curd to the sink and the refrigerator, respectively, and began to wash out the cups.

He finished, returned to his desk, and began to type. He'd barely added two paragraphs when the phone interrupted him. He finished the sentence and picked up the phone.

"Brandon?" he said. "Slow down, I can't understand you." After a long pause, he answered, "Of course you can come over right now. But what are you so flustered about?"

165

Mitch had to hold the phone away from his ear as Brandon sounded like a distressed chipmunk.

"It's not for a phone conversation?"

The chipmunk chattered on.

"Okay, I'll expect you in a little bit." He returned to his desk but had trouble focusing on his work. What could this be about? Brandon hadn't sounded upset, more confused and worried than anything. He shook himself and got back to work.

When the doorbell sounded, he was surprised, as he'd become so engrossed in his characters that it seemed only minutes since he'd been talking to Brandon on the phone.

"Hi," he said as he opened the door. "My, don't we look splendid in our new finery."

"Thanks to you, Mitch. I feel like a new person. All that guilt and remorse... gone. But now, of course, something else has come up."

"Sit down, and I'll get us some snacks." Brandon crossed to sit on the sofa as Mitch returned to the kitchen and soon came back with tea, and leftover crumpets.

"What are those, muffins?"

"These are authentic English crumpets, and the stuff in the jar is lemon curd. Em brought them to me this morning."

"The crumpets look great, but... lemon curd?" He mouthed the words with obvious distaste.

"Trust me. You'll love it. Tastes just like lemon meringue pie."

They both dug in with gusto.

"Now, tell me what's bothering you," Mitch said.

"Well, you won't believe me. How could this... this situation... become even more complicated?"

"Complicated?"

"I don't know quite how to say this. First, not a word to Sarah or Em, at least for now."

"Okay."

"Well... well.... David... sort of... came out to me."

"*What*?"

"Not so loud. Seems he's fought an attraction to guys all his life. But he didn't want to lose his mother's love and respect, so he never did anything about it. That's why he was so angry when he heard about her. Here he'd been hiding himself all these years so she wouldn't hate him, and she had similar feelings for women. He understands now, but at the time he was livid."

"Ye gods, complicated doesn't begin to describe this mess."

"There's more."

"More," Mitch exclaimed. "How could there be more?"

"Well… well, I think David is starting to have a thing for me."

Mitch slapped his hand against his forehead and moaned.

"And you?" he finally managed.

"Well… I… I think I'm starting to have a thing for David."

Mitch made a sound much like the "Arrrrgh" that Charlie Brown in *Peanuts* would exclaim when Lucy drove him crazy.

"That's why I had to come and see you, Mitch. I don't know what to do. The guy has done nothing with another man. Absolutely nothing. And I don't know if I'm capable of guiding him through this. The more I like him, the more afraid I am that I might cause him real harm."

Mitch was silent for a long time, as he thought things through.

"Bran," he said, finally. "I know you wouldn't hurt David. In fact, you'd probably be kinder about this than anybody I can think of."

"I was mean to you, Mitch."

"You were just doing your best to 'save me,' as you mistakenly thought you were supposed to do. You didn't want to hurt me."

"But…."

"Look, just take it slow. Let him get comfortable with himself, and, in his own time, he'll give you the opportunity to let him know how you feel. You can't desert him now. He's in a very delicate spot, and he really needs a solid presence to support him."

"He doesn't want his mother to know yet."

"That's all right. He'll come to terms with that on his own too. In the meantime, take him to the movies, out to dinner. Be a friend, and let the relationship grow into something more. That's my advice."

"You think so?"

"Be a little tactile with him. Not too much, just a pat on the back or a tap on the arm. Let him get used to you touching him. He probably craves that more than you know."

"Oh jeez, I'd love to do that, but wouldn't that be dangerous?"

"Not as long as you don't come on too strong. He's probably very shaky about his feelings and his actions. Just be patient, and be there for him. Let him know you care for him in subtle little ways. You know, fix a special dessert for him or something like that. I don't know what else to tell you. I'm probably not the best person to give advice on romance, you know."

"Oh, yes, you are. And I think I'll handle this just the way you suggested."

"Why don't you bring him to the little ceremony we're having for Em and Sarah, where they're going to repeat their vows. It's bound to be a very emotional moment, and maybe that'll break the ice."

"I'll ask, but I'm not sure if he's ready for that yet."

"You can only try."

Brandon left, and Mitch had trouble returning to his novel. But eventually he got caught up in the troubles of his characters, instead of his own.

IT WASN'T long before Mitch and Grady set out on a bright sunny morning on what would later become known as "The Great Party Store Crusade." On their way to the Party City on Fourteenth Street, they passed the recently closed St. Vincent's Hospital. Its obituary was printed in the newspapers on April 10.

"What a travesty," Mitch said bitterly.

"The poor thing even looks sad," Grady added.

"I have a friend who was an attending there, and he told me that as long as the doctors themselves were in charge, everything was fine. The minute the business people took over the administration, everything started going downhill."

"I've heard rumors that someone wants to turn it into a multilevel parking garage," Grady said.

"You're kidding."

"No. That's what I've heard. Apparently there was even a demonstration against it. The news trucks were here and everything."

"Well, it's murder is what it is. That hospital was very important, and they stuck a knife, or I should say a scalpel, into its heart."

"Very dramatic," Grady said, smiling.

Mitch said, "I am a master wordsmith, you know."

"Right," Grady said, giving Mitch a light slap on the back. Mitch warmed at the light touch. He found himself wanting Grady's hand to stay there.

As they rounded the corner at Fourteenth Street and started down the block, they agreed that it wouldn't be wise to stop by the Foot Locker store, to browse—just browse, mind you—for a few minutes. Likewise, the Starbucks that sat enticingly one shop before it. When they finally turned into Party City, Grady stopped in utter astonishment at the seemingly hundreds of balloons fastened onto the right wall all the way to the ceiling.

Mitch watched him, amused, likening Grady's reaction to that of a small boy getting his first view of Monkey Island at the zoo. Mitch was awed too, but then, he'd been to Party City before. One's first visit was rather startling, he realized.

There were balloons for every occasion in sizes from average to gigantic. Some were in the form of comic figures; there were Spider-Man, Cinderella, Barbie, the Little Mermaid, Batman and some unknown to man. Star shapes, shield shapes, round, square, some shaped like numbers: 16, 18, 21, 50, and 60 the most prominent. Countless ones for showers. On the ceiling above the counter were huge clusters of regular balloons waiting for customers to come pick them up, some in monotones, many pink or blue, and others of wild profusion. It was stupefying.

"I've never seen so many balloons in my life," Grady finally exclaimed. His eyes were… the only word that came to Mitch's mind was "shining."

"How about we get some clusters of regular white, and then two of those big ones that say 'Congratulations' in silver on a whitish background?" Mitch said.

"Whatever you think. I'm sort of numb. All ballooned out."

"Okay. We'll get them on the way out. There's more." Mitch took Grady's arm and led him down the large aisle to the right. He would have held on to his arm, it felt so good, but he didn't want Grady to guess his reason. They marveled at the boxes of costumes stacked high the full length of the left side of the aisle. There must have been a costume of every description in the world: ballerinas, policemen, soldiers, nurses, and too many princess outfits to number.

When they got to the adult section, Grady said, "How about you go as a pirate, and I'll go as a cowboy?" He then suggested more and more alternatives.

They cracked up, trying without much success to stifle their laughter. No such luck—a lot of the customers were staring at them. This proved to be even funnier to the two, and soon tears were running down their cheeks. They held on to each other to stay upright.

"This is a serious business," Mitch finally managed, wiping his cheeks.

"I know," Grady said. "That's what makes it so funny. The juxtaposition." They emitted a few leftover chuckles and continued on. They passed racks of swords, shields, feather boas, tiaras. There were table settings in every color, everything from tablecloths and napkins to complete place settings.

"Should we get some gold ones or silver?" Grady asked.

"Are you kidding? I'm bringing out the real thing. Crystal, china, sterling silver, the works."

"You have all that?"

"Well, yeah. I sort of inherited it."

Grady gave him a puzzled look.

"It all belonged to Jared's grandmother. I don't use it every day," he said, with a hint of embarrassment.

"Look," Grady interrupted, to get off the sad subject, "there are the accordion bells you wanted. I think that's them, at least. It's hard to tell when they're flat."

"Where?"

"Over there, by the piñatas." Grady pointed beyond several colorful shapes, including the traditional donkey. "Just beyond the big round pink one."

"Oh yeah," Mitch said. He hurried over, lifting one of the bells, and opened it up. It was huge and almost hit him in the face. That set Grady off laughing again.

"Dangerous, those wedding bells," he chided. "Be careful."

Mitch closed the bell, turned it around, and opened it toward Grady, who ducked around and came up behind Mitch. He grabbed another of the bells, opened it, and took a dueling stance.

"*En garde*," he said.

People were staring again. Mitch closed his bell.

"Nut," he said affectionately.

"As they say," Grady replied, "it takes one to know one."

They just stood there, each with a closed white bell, and stared at each other. God, but they were good together; the words they were both thinking were almost solid objects in the air. What great fun they had with each other. They could be totally nonsensical without any discomfort. They could see the funny side of things and really enjoy the vision. So in tune.

"Come on." Mitch finally broke the long silence. "Let's get a whole bunch of those rolls of white crepe paper. Then I think we've got everything." He tossed several rolls to Grady, who caught them expertly, and then he took some for himself.

The struggle home, loaded with the helium-filled balloons and bags of bells and paper and other paraphernalia, became part of the legend of the Great Party Store Crusade.

THE PREPARATIONS for Em and Sarah's wedding vows moved along fairly well. Now the big day was here, and the ceiling was festooned with streamers arced from bell to bell in great twisted loops. Grady had managed to find a bolt of white satin and had draped the fireplace into a kind of altar. They'd found white candles with thin gold spirals from bottom to top for the Christofle candlesticks and a proper wedding cake topped by two brides, which had been delivered that morning. The oak kitchen table, with all its leaves put in, had been moved to the living room and looked resplendent with Mitch's best linen, silver, and glassware. Puppy even had a large white bow around his neck and had promised to be a good boy. (If he couldn't contain himself, he would spend the time of the ceremony contemplating his behavior in the bedroom.) Mitch and Grady were both rather resplendent in dark blue suits. Yes, everything was coming together nicely.

When the doorbell rang, Mitch hurried to open it. "I hope this isn't the brides, who've become too anxious to wait until the appointed time."

"Well, you know Em," Grady said resignedly.

But when Mitch opened the door, it was Brandon—and behind him stood a slightly uncertain David.

"Brandon, you made it. And, David, I'm so glad you came too."

"I didn't pressure him," Brandon said quickly as they entered.

"No," David said. "I've learned a lot these last few days, and I wouldn't want to miss one of the most important days in my mother's life."

"She'll be absolutely delighted," Grady said.

"Where are we supposed to stand?" Brandon asked.

"Well, I'm standing with Em, a few steps back, however, and I think it only right for David to do the same for Sarah."

"Oh, no," David said. "I think Grady should...."

"Brandon will stand to your side, and I'll stand beside Mitch," Grady added.

"But—"

"Besides, I have to hold Puppy. He wouldn't want to miss anything," Grady said.

When he heard his name, Puppy peeked out from beneath the tablecloth, where he'd spent most of the morning, as if he understood that big doings where taking place. They could hear his tail thumping on the floor. Then he pulled back into his little cave, as if he needed his rest.

"It's time," Mitch said after looking at his watch. He quickly turned on the CD player, where he'd placed an Erik Satie collection, and the air was filled with a beautiful, peaceful piece he thought appropriate for the moment. It had just started when a soft knock at the door froze everyone for a moment. Mitch wasn't used to this sound purportedly from Em. He opened the door, and the two brides entered.

Such splendor! Sarah was wearing a light blue lace dress, a little hat with a blue veil to match her dress, and gloves and shoes of a darker blue. Em shocked them all be appearing in a rich royal blue satin pantsuit. She'd obviously purchased a brand-new wig, a soft brown with a few streaks of gray in it. Both had bouquets of white carnations and roses. (Mitch had sent them earlier.)

Now, Mitch stepped forward and offered Em his arm. He motioned for David to do likewise, which he did, offering Sarah his arm. Sarah was having a difficult time managing the bouquet and the little lace handkerchief that had appeared when she saw David in the room. The two couples walked slowly toward the satin-draped altar. Grady had hurried to pick Puppy up and now held him in his arms. Mitch took a few steps ahead and turned to face the others.

"We're here today to bear witness to the vows of our loved ones, Em and Sarah. In our privileged company, they will pledge their devotion to each other, each in her own words." He stepped back into place.

"Fortune has really smiled on me," Em began in a low shaky voice. "For I've found for the second time a wonderful woman to share my life with. I thought I was to go on alone. But… well… then came my dear Sarah, and… and our future…." She shook her head, unable to go on.

Sarah smiled at her and came to her rescue by starting her own speech. "I've led a very happy life, as my dear boy standing here can attest. But now I have an added happiness I never thought I'd know. And this sweet, unpredictable woman is responsible. Em, we'll go on through the years together."

Mitch was shocked to see tears slipping down Em's cheeks as Sarah proceeded to hug her. They exchanged a quick kiss and then turned with radiant smiles to the others. Mitch produced a scroll that he and Grady had designed, spelling out their vows, and the four young men signed it as witness to the event. Mitch had put a little ink on Puppy's paw and added it to their signatures.

The champagne flowed, the sumptuous meal was devoured, the wedding cake destroyed, and a very good time was had by all.

However, when they were finally left alone, Mitch and Grady flopped on the sofa, each at his own end. As sleep pulled them under, Mitch managed to croak, "What did you think?"

Grady's answer was almost inaudible. "So happy for them, but what I felt mostly was envy." And then he slept.

Mitch, however, was now wide-awake.

Chapter Ten

THEN THE dreadful day was upon them—the day of Grady's departure. Mitch had tossed and turned all night, never falling completely into a deep sleep. He was overcome with a feeling of the deepest dread. It seemed as if someone were going to pull off an arm or a leg; the feeling was that fierce. There was no longer any question in his mind; he was in love with Grady. Deeply, powerfully in love. And should he, could he, let Grady go off without saying something? To say something at this late date would be incredibly awkward... and rushed. A declaration such as this should be given in an intense but quiet moment, not blurted out just as Grady went out the door. What to do?

He'd been in and out of Grady's room dozens of times, watching him pack until he thought his head might explode, and he had to leave the room, only to wander back within a few moments. He somehow needed to be in Grady's presence, as if he might never have it again. And that felt to him like the end of the world.

"Well," Grady said, clicking his suitcase shut, "I guess that's it. I know I've forgotten something, but you can always send it to me, or better yet, bring it up in person." He smiled.

Mitch's breath caught, and he was only able to nod.

Grady picked up the suitcase and passed Mitch, heading toward the front door. Mitch was frantic. He didn't know quite what to say, what to do. He felt a life-changing moment was upon him, and he must somehow crank up the nerve to act upon it. So difficult. So necessary. He followed Grady out into the living room.

Grady said, "I guess, the big moment is here. I have the worst case of separation anxiety. It's crazy."

"If that makes you crazy, then I am too."

Just as Grady got to the door and was about to open it, Mitch strode forward and stopped him with a hand on his shoulder, turning him around. He took the suitcase from his hand and put it on the floor. He took in the puzzled look on Grady's face, and after a moment's hesitation when he almost stepped back, he put his hands on Grady's cheeks, leaned forward, and let their lips touch.

Oh God, what if Grady pulled away. He'd die! What if Grady thought he was taking advantage of him? What if... he....

Grady deepened the kiss, put his arms around Mitch, and pulled him close. Mitch's mind exploded into a kaleidoscope of vivid colors, at once aware of the soft texture of Grady's lips, the strength of his muscles, and the hardness below Grady's waist pressing insistently against Mitch's own. They pressed together as close as was humanly possible and began moving against each other as they both made soft moaning noises.

Within seconds a great wave of pleasure swept up Mitch's spine as his orgasm nearly split him apart. He could feel the several shocks in Grady's body, and he knew they'd both climaxed at the same time. Finally, Mitch pulled back and stared into the deep pools Grady's eyes had become.

"That," he whispered, "was—I'm ecstatic!"

"Ah, Mitch," Grady replied, "I've wanted this to happen for so long. You've become the most important thing in my life, and I was afraid I'd spoil our friendship if I tried to take things further."

"It's my fault. I've always been so afraid of being hurt again. I'd cut myself off from feeling anything for anyone. What an idiot."

"No, you're the most incredible guy I've ever known... not to mention the best-looking."

"Aw, Grady, you're so sweet. How could anyone not fall for you? I did in spite of myself."

Just then a loud honking broke in from down in the street.

"Oh no, that's my ride."

"Hideous timing," Mitch told him.

"You know it," Grady replied, stepping back from Mitch. "Tell them I'll be right down. I've got to get cleaned up and put on fresh clothes."

As he passed, Mitch grabbed him and kissed him again. "We certainly made a mess, didn't we?"

"Yeah, but such a good one. We're like a couple of kids having their first experience. You know, like a spacecraft warning… seconds to blast off."

Laughing, Grady ran into his bedroom. Mitch went to the window and called down that Grady wasn't quite through packing and that he needed a bit more time.

But one of the guys down below called back up, "Tell him to take his time. We just decided to get some lunch, so we'll come back for him in about half an hour."

"Great!" Mitch called back, his blood suddenly racing through his system like a flash flood. He ran back to Grady's bedroom to find Grady standing there, sans clothes and holding a blue towel loosely in his hand. The result of their recent encounter was quite visible on his abs.

"They're going to lunch and won't be back for about half an hour."

Mitch started tearing his clothes off, until he was in his natural state, like Grady. He saw Grady grinning at him and, following his gaze, saw that his own stomach was covered with the same white, viscous mess.

That didn't stop Mitch from crossing the room, taking Grady in his arms, and pulling their bodies together. They couldn't seem to help sliding back and forth in the slick, smooth fluid still pooled on their bodies. The sensation was too much, and all their pent-up longing volcanoed in simultaneous eruptions, adding warm new lubrication to what was already there. They clung to each other, enjoying the sensual pleasure of the satiny smooth feeling of the fluid they'd created between them. Just as Mitch was about to say something, they heard the raucous honking of the car horn again.

"Guess they decided to skip lunch," Mitch said. "Damn."

"No time for a shower," Grady said, wiping himself off with the blue towel he still clutched in his hand. When he finished he handed the towel to Mitch. "Hope there's enough dry space for you." Grady pulled on fresh worn Levi's and a white T-shirt.

"Don't need it," Mitch replied.

"What?"

"I want to savor the moment for a little while. I want to be able to feel the proof."

"Devil," Grady said, smiling broadly. He grabbed his bag and gave Mitch a quick but slightly distant hug. Then he was gone, and Mitch ran his hand over his abs, remembering, and thinking about what they might accomplish in the future, given more time. He smiled.

MITCH FELT the lonely days trudge by as if he were walking through glue. He'd relived Grady's departure over and over again. Neither of them referred to it in their constant phone calls. It was as if they'd both decided that the moment was too important to discuss in any way but in person, face-to-face. And while Mitch felt that Grady's phone calls were the only thing that kept him from flying apart, they were a gossamer thing compared to Grady's presence. Puppy was a great comfort, his little pal. Mitch could always count on Puppy's antics to keep him from falling into too deep a gloom. Puppy loved to play let's-pull-on-the-rope with Mitch. However, when Mitch let him win and tug the rope away, Puppy actually looked disappointed, as if to say that was not the way the game was played, and he would let go of his end too and just look at Mitch with a questioning expression on his face. Then, when Mitch grabbed for the rope, Puppy was right there, snapping up his end and pulling for all he was worth. Mitch caught himself actually laughing many times.

They were playing a heated such game when the phone rang. Mitch had gotten so his sprits went soaring when the phone rang; it just might be Grady calling

"Hi," he said, suddenly happy when it was, indeed, Grady, "are you all ready for opening night?"

"Don't scare me to death," Grady said. "I've got two more days before that happens."

"I'll bet you look adorable in your little blue-striped suit."

"I do not look adorable. I look stupid."

"No. Definitely adorable. Remember, I've seen the costume sketches, and I can vividly imagine you in that suit."

"Well, one good thing—you won't have to imagine me with a mustache. They've decided against it."

"I know you hated the idea."

"There wasn't time to grow a real one, and a fake one always has at least one wild hair that goes right up your nose and drives you crazy throughout the whole performance."

Mitch chuckled, picturing Grady standing outdoors, his phone to his ear, with green trees in the background and a dimming sky behind him. If only he could be there too.

"You're still coming for opening night?" Grady asked.

"Of course. Nothing would keep me from it. Em and Sarah are almost giddy with anticipation. And Brandon and David may come too."

"Oh my God, the whole posse."

"Your own rooting section."

"I'll make reservations, so you'll all have good seats."

"That's thinking ahead. It didn't occur to me."

"Sorry, I have to go now. They're having a run-through... without costumes, thank heavens."

"No little blue suit?"

"No little blue suit."

"Okay. You take care, Grady."

"You too, love."

And Grady hung up quickly, the last word almost lost.

Mitch sat right down on the floor, absently holding the receiver in his hand. His legs simply wouldn't hold him up. Had he imagined it? No, he was sure that was what Grady had said. Wow, the power of words! He felt numb all over. The phone broke through his haze with its sharp reminder that it was off the hook. He struggled up and replaced the receiver. Puppy ran over, and Mitch picked him up.

"Puppy, what do you think Grady just said?" he asked.

179

Puppy licked his chin.

"Right. You're one smart puppy, Puppy. He said the big *L* word."

Grinning, he slumped down onto the sofa with Puppy cuddled warmly on his chest and was soon lost in deep contemplation.

THE RIDE up to the theater on opening night was one big blur to Mitch. Highway, trees, red lights, white lights, trees, water, trees, trees, trees, bridge, highway, trees, vague shapes that must be other cars, trees, trees, trees.

Sarah, David, and Brandon sat in the backseat, and Em sat beside him in front, their conversations muted mumblings. He was sure he was answering Em's questions and commenting on her remarks, but he didn't have the faintest idea what he was saying.

And then they were pulling into the parking lot. A large asphalt area surrounded the barnlike structure. Painted red with white trim, the theater stood on a small hill looking over the surrounding greenery and the scattered lights of residences nearby. Some of the audience members were already streaming in and out of the theater, collecting in small groups and talking. It was a balmy evening with a slight breeze. The fresh, earthy smell of the country was delightful to the five city dwellers.

"I'll go get our tickets," Mitch said. "You might as well enjoy the evening air until it's curtain time. I'll be right back."

"Hope you can remember where we are, Foggy," Em quipped.

"Now, Em," Sarah cautioned.

Mitch barely heard them as he hurried over the rough, uneven pavement toward the main entrance. As he entered, he saw that once again photos of the cast were prominently displayed. His gaze zeroed in on Grady's photo. Just as handsome as always. There was a scattering of rehearsal shots, some in costume. Mitch stopped long enough to scan these briefly. Yes, Grady was adorable in the little blue suit! The girl playing Carrie was wearing a blue dress with white trim. They looked like a matched set of dolls.

Mitch looked up and saw programs in frames from older productions surrounding the lobby on a rack closer to the ceiling. This theater had done an astounding number of plays.

He moved through the crowd toward the box office. Of course there was a line. For no reason at all, he was very impatient. He kept wanting to say, "Hurry up." He could hardly wait for the sight of Grady on stage. Finally, his turn came. He looked through the gilded bars and mentioned Grady's name to the pleasant-looking older woman who commanded the box office.

"Five for Mr. Snow's family, right?"

"Yes," Mitch replied. "We're here in force."

"That's wonderful. Our Mr. Snow is a real dear."

"Don't I know it," Mitch said.

She smiled and handed him the envelope with the tickets.

"We're starting soon," she told him. "You don't want to miss the overture."

"Thanks, I'll gather the troops."

Mitch hurried back, tossed a "found you easy" to Em, and led them back to the theater. They found Grady had reserved five seats in the very front row. The theater had Continental seating, which meant a large center section with an aisle on either side with smaller seating sections to the left and right. The lush red-plush seating was very comfortable and roomy. The first row was separated from the raised stage by the orchestra, two grand pianos, a bass and drums. The curtain was a deep scarlet and was subtly lit in artistic light and shadowed sections. The orchestra began the overture, which, of course, Mitch had heard so many times in his living room that he knew every note. But it was so much fuller with the added instruments. He shivered in anticipation.

The scenes flew by and then, finally, Mr. Snow and Carrie began their duet, "When The Children Are Asleep." Grady's voice was sonorous, and the girl playing Carrie matched him well. How could the evil Iago so easily turn into the naïve fisherman, Mr. Snow? Grady was, indeed, a fine actor.

Then it was all over, and the cast was coming onstage for their curtain call. The audience seemed to rise as one. A standing ovation!

As Mitch jumped to his feet, he saw Grady looking down at him with a huge smile on his face. To Mitch it was as if someone had turned the sun on. The cast took five curtain calls before the audience reluctantly let them leave the stage.

Out in the lobby, where the cast was receiving their admirers, Mitch found a crowd of strangers complimenting Grady. Each actor had similar groups of fans. When Grady was finally free, Mitch stepped forward and pulled him into a hug.

"Careful," Grady said, "you'll get makeup all over you."

"Don't care," Mitch answered. As he pulled away, he let his lips graze Grady's cheek. If Grady could risk the *L* word, Mitch could risk that much.

Then it was hugs from all the others, and many compliments. Grady thanked Sarah especially for all her help with the music.

"I've never before felt so secure with the music in a show. They all thought I was some kind of musical prodigy, but I told them I had an excellent coach."

"Just a little help," Sarah said, blushing furiously with pleasure.

"It was a lot," Grady insisted. "I'm sorry, we have notes from the director, and then we have to go over some trouble spots. It could be hours. I wish we could go somewhere for a bite to eat, but I have to stay here."

"That's all right," Mitch fibbed. "We'll just go on home and live this terrific night over again on the way."

"It meant a lot to me having you in the audience tonight," Grady told them as someone called urgently for him to come away. "So long," he said as he trotted off, waving over his shoulder.

They threw their congratulations and good-byes after him like verbal confetti.

The ride home was very quiet. Em and Sarah both fell asleep. Mitch was lost in thought, with visions of little blue suits dancing in his head.

MITCH WAS rather frantic the next day after being so close to Grady and then having to leave so suddenly. Everything felt so... so...

unfinished. By the day after that, he'd decided what to do. He would somehow finagle the car and drive up to the theater alone. Once there he would get Grady alone and declare himself. He would offer love and lifelong commitment. Hopefully Grady would feel the same way; it certainly seemed that would be his response. He couldn't imagine life now without Grady. That would be unendurable. This small separation had shown him that.

After a feeble but successful excuse, he borrowed Em's car. He'd phoned the theater and made himself a reservation. He knew if he mentioned the trip, the rest of the family would all want to accompany him. He needed to be alone. Alone with Grady. After the show, no matter how late, they would talk. The drive up to the theater was, if anything, more of a blur than the first time. He arrived at the theater a little early; curtain time was at least fifteen minutes off. Mitch didn't want Grady to see him until the show was over, so he wandered around the theater parking lot. As he rounded a corner, as far away as he could get from the theater itself, through a dense tangle of trees he was just able to glimpse part of a small porch where a couple of actors were talking. Suddenly he recognized the little blue suit. It was Grady and the fellow who'd played Billy, the lead. Mitch smiled and hid himself as he watched the two talking animatedly. Then—then Grady pulled the other man to him, and they kissed passionately. The other man flung his arms around Grady and pulled him close. The kiss intensified.

Kiss… kiss…. Grady kissing another man… impossible… before his eyes… no, not Grady… still kissing….

Mitch suddenly saw nothing but blackness. He'd squeezed his eyes shut so hard they hurt. He wanted to scream. He wanted to howl. He… he… wanted to… die. He staggered back against one of the cars. Now his sight was all blurry. No… no… not again. Could he survive losing his love twice? Then all thought passed away. He wasn't certain he remained conscious, but suddenly he was aware of the rough, black ground beneath his feet. Now his feet were actually moving. Where? Oh, toward his car. He was in the car. He was starting the ignition. He was driving away. He was on the way back. Back… back to… what?

Mitch never knew how he got home. He found he'd garaged the car and was now standing in the middle of his apartment. He was cold, so cold. He shivered. Puppy ambled over and nipped at his ankles. He picked Puppy up, and, slumping on the sofa, he buried his face in Puppy's fur. He felt a bit comforted by the warm softness. What was he going to do? How would he get through his days? Grady… thinking the very name caused him to ache. He thought he knew Grady. How could he have been so mistaken?

Mitch fell asleep on the sofa, anything to avoid thinking, feeling. How long he lay there he didn't know, but when he woke up, Puppy was gone, and someone was ringing the bell. It had to be Em. It was her ring. Then came loud knocking. Em, for sure. He didn't answer. He didn't want to see anyone. He trudged into the bedroom, threw himself on the bed, and promptly fell asleep again. Dreamless. Lost. Nowhere.

The next time he surfaced, it was to Puppy making strange little noises. Hungry. The poor little thing was hungry. How long had it been? Mitch had been unable to eat anything. He looked gaunt and unshaven, rumpled and bleary-eyed. He staggered to his feet and went into the kitchen, trying to avoid Puppy's accusing eyes. He poured out some puppy food and filled the water dish. Puppy actually pushed his hand away and began to gobble his dinner.

"Sorry, Puppy," Mitch said, sitting on the floor. "Forgive me?"

Apparently, Puppy did, because when he was finished he trotted over and plopped himself on Mitch's lap. Mitch ran his hand over Puppy's slick fur absently.

"Ah, Puppy, where do we go from here?"

Mitch remembered gathering up all Grady's belongings and piling them outside the front door in the hall with a note to Em to keep them until Grady got back, so she could pass them on when Grady found a new place to live.

He'd felt almost drunk when he'd done that, but he couldn't bear stumbling onto all those signs of Grady at every turn. In one black cloud he'd grabbed everything he could find of Grady's and put it all in the hall. Out of sight, out of mind… right? Wrong… but a little bit better.

Mitch figured, through a fog, that Em must have found the pile of stuff and the note he'd left for Grady. Her knocking on his door seemed likely to break it down.

"You open this door," she hollered. "Talk to me, Mitch. For heaven's sake, what's wrong?"

"Just leave me alone, Em. Please. Just go away."

"Why won't you talk to me? I'm so worried about you, Mitch."

"I'm sorry, Em. I don't want to see anyone right now. Later… later, we'll talk."

"As your friend, I'll leave you alone for a while. As your landlady, pretty soon I'm going to use my pass key and drag you out of there… by the hair, if necessary!"

"Deal," Mitch said. "But for now, just please leave me alone."

Then had come the phone calls from Grady. And the knocks on the door. His voice on Mitch's answering machine sounded so lost. He kept asking what was wrong, what had happened. Mitch worked desperately to turn his heart into a stone. Despite longing to do otherwise, he refused to answer. Finally he unplugged the phone.

When the pounding on the door became unbearable, Mitch had yelled. "Dammit, Grady, leave me alone. Just go away!"

And then all was quiet for a time.

Now he heard a soft knocking on his door. Almost a scratching noise. Ah well, time to face somebody. He got up, put Puppy down, and shambled over to the door.

"Have you got a cup of tea for a friend?" Sarah asked quietly.

The gentle Sarah. How could he turn her away?

"I poured out my heart to you, Mitch. Can't you do likewise with me?"

He held the door open.

Sarah entered and went to sit on the sofa, much like she had that first time.

"Chamomile tea would be nice," she said.

Shrugging, Mitch gave in to the inevitable.

He fixed the tea and returned with the same tray and cups and saucers as they'd used in their talk, which seemed so long ago.

He gestured for her to pour, which she did expertly. Then she took her cup and sat back.

"Dear, what's wrong? You look miserable. And Grady's in the same shape downstairs. He doesn't understand what's happened. He says you won't talk to him either. That's not fair. At least tell me what's bothering you."

"Ah, Sarah…."

"Drink your tea, and then… just tell me. Remember I was able to tell you something I'd never told anyone. And I barely knew you. Can't you give me that same kind of trust?"

"Sarah… I just don't know what to do. I'm totally lost. Everything… everything… is just…."

"Go on. That's a start," she encouraged him.

"I drove up to the theater the night after opening. I didn't tell anyone. I wanted to talk to Grady alone."

"Em figured out that's what you were up to."

"She's too smart for her own good."

"That's debatable… but we won't talk about that right now."

"Anyway, I got there early, and I was walking around the parking lot when I saw Grady and the guy who played the lead, Billy. And… and…."

"And?" she prompted.

"They—" he whispered. "They were… kissing."

"Kissing? No."

"Yes. I couldn't believe my eyes. I think I was certifiable for a time. I don't remember much until I got home. I remember picking Puppy up and falling asleep on the sofa. I'm… I'm crushed, Sarah. Literally. I feel like I don't exist anymore."

"Oh, my dear," Sarah said, taking his hand. "I'm so sorry. Are you sure there isn't some explanation? That doesn't sound at all like the Grady we know."

"It sure doesn't. But I saw him."

"I know, dear. That must have hurt you a lot. But let me go down and ask him about it. Would that be all right? If I ask about it?"

"Sure. Why not? What could make this worse?"

"Now you just have some more tea… it's very good at times like this."

She stood up, and he stood with her. She hugged him and left.

Mitch finished the tea. It didn't seem to help much. He was starting to fall asleep again.

He jumped at the pounding on his door. This was louder than anything Em had ever produced. It seemed like the door would split apart.

"Mitch," he heard Grady hollering. "You open this door right now, or I swear to God I'll break the damned thing in. Mitch! Come on now! Open the damned door!"

The pounding got even fiercer.

Mitch staggered to the door and opened it.

There stood a beleaguered and haunted-looking Grady. He didn't seem angry so much as frustrated. He pulled Mitch into his arms. Mitch fell against him, limp, without any anger at all.

It didn't seem to matter that Grady had deceived him. He realized that in spite of everything that had happened, he still loved the man.

"You fool," Grady said softly. "You foolish, foolish man." He pulled back until they were facing each other.

"That kiss was part of the new play I told you about. I'd already signed the contract. It was too late to get somebody else. I never would have signed it if I'd known there was a kiss involved. The only way I got through it was to pretend it was you. The director was right there on the porch, insisting we go rehearse it again. He said in performance, my face couldn't look like I was tasting poison, and I had to stop it. He kept insisting and—"

"I… I didn't see anybody else there… there were so many trees in the way."

"You only saw the two of us? Oh, my poor Mitch." Grady squeezed him so tightly he could hardly breathe.

When he finally could, he said, "Grady, how… how could I ever… have… have mistrusted you? I should have known you'd never…."

"I would have told you about it, but I felt so guilty. Even though the whole deal was out of my hands, I felt like I was betraying you. It was agony."

"And I made it worse."

"I just couldn't figure out what went wrong. Everything seemed so perfect, and then I came back, and you wouldn't even talk to me."

"It was that horrible feeling of loss I'd felt after what happened to Jared. Old buttons got pushed. I hardly knew what I was doing."

"Me too."

"You called it right: I've been a fool."

"No. Just confused and that's—"

"Well, I'm not confused anymore!"

"God, I hope not."

"I love you, Grady, with all my heart."

"And I love you right back, Mitch. With everything I've got."

"We're so lucky."

"I felt so damn alone, Mitch, without you."

"Me too, Grady."

And, faintly, as if from some great distance, Mitch heard Ella Fitzgerald once again singing that plaintive little song, "All By Myself…."

Not anymore, Mitch thought with great joy. *Never again.*

KEN BACHTOLD graduated from San Francisco State University with a BA and an MA in acting and directing and a minor in art. Passing up a great teaching job and surrendering to the "lure of the big time" he came to New York. After pounding the pavement, as it were, and finding it wanting, he decided to shape his own destiny and founded A Company Of Players Repertory Theatre, and then produced and directed five plays, including J.M. Barrie's *Dear Brutus*. For The Drama Committee he directed several plays including Oscar Wilde's *An Ideal Husband* and *A Woman Of No Importance*. He wrote and directed the musical *Saloon*, based loosely on *The Drunkard*, which opened a brand new dinner theater in New Jersey and received rave reviews. Being accepted at the BMI Musical Comedy Class, he wrote *The Facts Of Life*. Two other original musicals include *Boo!* and *Dilemma!*

He acted in and directed many shows for Frank Calo's ongoing Spotlight On Festivals, Inc., including Jean Anouilh's *Antigone*. More recently he wrote and directed the gay-themed original play *Starting Over*, accepted for the Ninth Annual Fresh Fruit Festival.

Always an avid reader, his two-year-old Kindle currently stores 400 books, mostly MM romance. Often frustrated at finding exactly the type of story he favored, he thought, "What the hell, I should write one." And so he did! Naturally, he was profoundly delighted when it was accepted for publication by Dreamspinner Press. He hopes you like it!

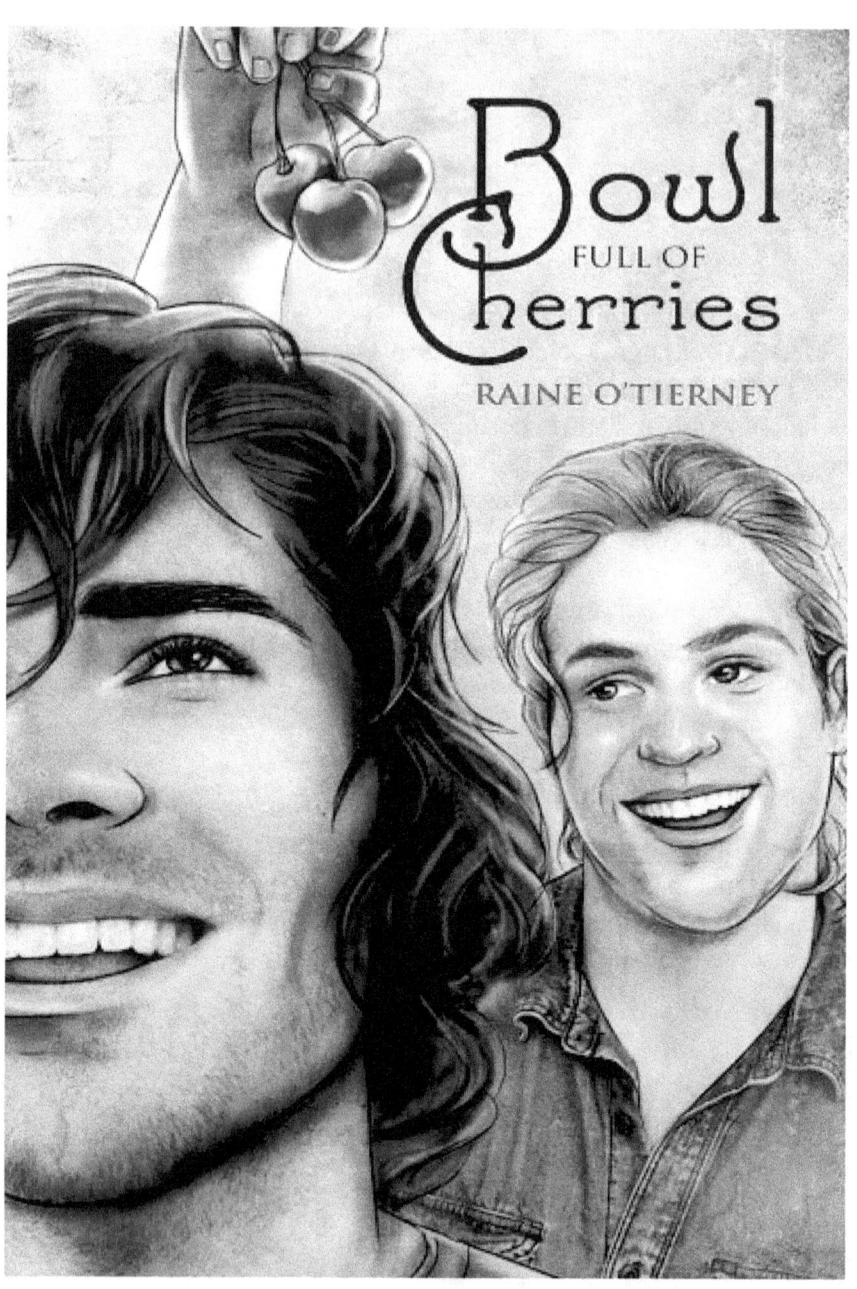

Bowl
FULL OF
Cherries

RAINE O'TIERNEY

http://www.dreamspinnerpress.com

Kate Sherwood

IN TOO DEEP

http://www.dreamspinnerpress.com

RENAE
KAYE

SAFE
IN HIS
ARMS

http://www.dreamspinnerpress.com

All That *HEAVEN* Will Allow

D.W. MARCHWELL

http://www.dreamspinnerpress.com